"We need to talk about what happened, Sadie."

"I've been thinking about it, too," she admitted, hoping Isaac hadn't noticed the crack in her voice.

His posture straightened as if he was putting on the bravest front that he could muster. "Saying that I had nothing keeping me here was a poor choice of words. I think you took that to mean that our friendship isn't worth moving for, and that is far from the truth."

Isaac reached for Sadie's hand and held it securely, his brown eyes gazing directly into hers. "You mean the world to me, Sadie. Truly, you do."

"*Jah*, you mean an awful lot to me as well," Sadie replied breathily. There was no denying it now—she was developing feelings for the man whom she was courting for the sake of convenience. What a mess this was. She couldn't pine over someone who would never truly be hers, even if Isaac was the kindest, most understanding and handsome man she'd ever met…

Jackie Stef began immersing herself in Amish culture at a young age and wrote her first Amish story at eleven years old. When she's not busy writing, she enjoys photography, playing with her pets and exploring the back roads of Lancaster County. She lives in rural Pennsylvania and loves to spend time in nature.

Books by Jackie Stef

Love Inspired

Their Make-Believe Match

Visit the Author Profile page at LoveInspired.com.

Their Make-Believe Match

Jackie Stef

LOVE INSPIRED
INSPIRATIONAL ROMANCE

LOVE INSPIRED®

INSPIRATIONAL ROMANCE

Recycling programs
for this product may
not exist in your area.

ISBN-13: 978-1-335-58513-4

Their Make-Believe Match

Love Inspired
22 Adelaide St. West, 41st Floor
Toronto, Ontario M5H 4E3, Canada
www.LoveInspired.com

Printed in U.S.A.

Trust in the Lord with all thine heart;
and lean not unto thine own understanding.
In all thy ways acknowledge him,
and he shall direct thy paths.
—*Proverbs* 3:5–6

This book is dedicated to
my wonderful parents, Diane and Mark Stefanowicz,
who have always supported my dream
of becoming an author.

Thank you to Angel Milazzo and Mekaelah Moray,
two of my close friends who encouraged me
and helped me brainstorm when writer's block hit.
(And it hits quite often!)

A special thank-you also to Tamela Hancock Murray,
my literary agent, and Melissa Endlich, my editor;
thank you for believing in me!

to daydream about something that would likely never happen wouldn't help her finish her work.

As she hosed the dirty water off her feet and flip-flops, Sadie's heart warmed at the sound of the flirtatious laughter of the couple while they circled the entirety of the greenhouse. Sadie grinned, knowing that she couldn't judge them for doing such a thing. She also took time to stop and smell the roses, more often than not.

I imagine some would say that's why I've been passed over for courting, Sadie mused as she coiled the hose around the crook of her arm and then placed it on its holder. She fought off the notion of inadequacy as a woman and mentally pushed past her longing for love and a family of her own.

Perhaps it was her direct social nature, but more than likely it was her fierce independence and almost childlike zest for life that seemed to have scared away the young men in her community. Even her parents occasionally reminded her not to be stubborn and immature. They'd recently threatened to fix her up with an eligible bachelor if she couldn't find a husband of her own. Absolutely appalled by the idea of matchmaking, Sadie knew that time was running out for her to find a suitor on her own. But finding a man who understood her outlook on life seemed about as unlikely as cats and dogs literally raining from above.

No reason to fret, she reminded herself half-heartedly. *If the Lord wills me to find someone special, He'll pave the way*. Still, the notion that the eligible men in her community found her to be too much to handle threatened to shout at Sadie more loudly than the heavy drumming of the rain on the greenhouse roof.

By the time Sadie swept up the loose soil around the self-serve potting station and assisted a few customers at the cash register, her workday had come to an end. She bid goodbye to her coworkers before making her way to the exit. She thoroughly enjoyed tending to the plants and assisting the patrons, but briefly thinking about what she was missing in her life had knocked the wind out of her sails. The vision of Rhoda's horse and buggy waiting for her in the parking lot would be a sight for sore eyes. Hitching a ride home with soft-spoken Rhoda, her dearest friend since childhood, was often the highlight of Sadie's day. Time spent with her closest companion was always cherished, as were the day-old pastries Rhoda shared from her work at the nearby bakery.

Sadie exited the greenhouse and her eyes widened with surprise. She knew it had been raining throughout the day and had often paused to marvel at the seeming millions of droplets racing down the sides of the greenhouse's windowpanes, but she hadn't realized that the steady rain had morphed into a downright deluge. Squinting into the spray of water that seemed to be blowing sideways, she dashed through the downpour and made a beeline toward Rhoda's waiting buggy. *Thank goodness she's here on time.* Sadie grinned to herself as raindrops pelted her face.

With gusto, Sadie's running start had her jumping over a puddle and launching herself into Rhoda's buggy. When she'd situated herself in the passenger's seat, Sadie glanced at her reflection in the side mirror. "Well, don't I look like a wet noodle." She poked at her sheer, heart-shaped head covering, which now lay limply on top of her blond head. "Doesn't that look like a dead fish?" She flicked the *kapp* to make it jiggle and then burst into a fit of hearty laughter.

When Rhoda didn't laugh, Sadie turned to face her friend and let out a gasp. Instead of the familiar female face, she was shocked to see a startled young Amish man staring at her with a curious expression. She had mistakenly entered a stranger's buggy!

Sadie's hand flew to her chest to still her racing heart as she studied the handsome fellow, who was clearly just as surprised as she was. The style of his straw hat differed from the kind Amish men in Lancaster wore. *He must be from out of town.* His drenched sky blue shirt clung to his muscular frame, hard evidence that he, too, had been caught in the rain. A bit of sadness hid behind his bewildered expression, and something within Sadie's heart longed to see this stranger smile.

"Well, you certainly aren't Rhoda," Sadie declared with a playful smirk.

A small grin crossed the fellow's lips. "*Nee*, I'm definitely not Rhoda."

"Didn't think so." Sadie chuckled as she leaned against the seat. "You don't mind if I keep you company, do you?"

The stunned stranger stared at her in obvious confusion. "What?"

Sadie reworded her request. "Do you mind if I sit here while I wait for my friend to show up? My shift at the greenhouse is over, so I ran out here thinking that this was her buggy." She peeked into the parking lot and scanned their surroundings. "Yours is the only buggy parked out here, ain't so?"

"I don't mind at all," the man replied with a slight shake of his tilted head, as if curious as to why a young lady would so willingly sit alone with a stranger.

Truth be told, Sadie felt safe with a fellow Amish person, regardless of whether they had previously met or not. Sadie glanced at the young man, who seemed so down that she wondered if she'd been led to seek shelter in his buggy. *He looks like he needs a friend.*

"We should introduce ourselves. I can't seem to place your face," Sadie suggested, eager to learn more about the good-looking stranger.

The man smiled, seemingly amused by her direct-ness. "I'm Isaac Hostettler. My *mamm* and I moved here from Indiana just yesterday."

Sadie leaned forward, causing rain droplets from the top of her head to run down to the tip of her nose. "That's quite the journey, *jah*? What made you choose to move to Bird-in-Hand?"

Isaac's cute smile vanished as he reached for the horse's reins, perhaps out of nervousness. "My *mamm* hasn't been feelin' so good lately, so we came to live with my aunt, Miriam Fisher, in hopes that it would lift *Mamm's* spirits." One of his shoulders shrugged as if he didn't have the enthusiasm to move both. "The change of scenery, you know?"

Sadie let out a pained sigh, her heart aching for her

new acquaintance. "I'm so sorry to hear your *mamm* is sick. That must be awful hard on both of you."

"Oh, she's not sick," Isaac corrected Sadie, his tanned face rapidly turning pale. "Someone we loved passed away, and it was…very hard for all of us and—"

"I understand," Sadie mercifully interrupted, "you don't have to say any more." She reached for his hand and gave it a reassuring pat. She sensed that a comforting gesture was just what Isaac needed. The brief touch of her hand against his gave her butterflies in her stomach that she did her best to ignore.

Isaac shook his head, letting out a sigh that sounded more like a laugh. "You speak to me like we're old friends." A weak but genuine smile spread across his lips. "I'm glad you clambered into my buggy."

"Well, we are friends now, aren't we?" Sadie asked with a quirked eyebrow.

"*Jah*, and I'm glad." Isaac nodded, studying her as if she were the most compelling creature he'd ever laid eyes on.

Sadie was unsure of what to say or do next as silence settled between them. Without thinking, she puffed out her rosy cheeks and crossed her emerald eyes as Isaac continued to stare at her.

Obviously taken aback by Sadie's unexpected silliness, Isaac squinted at her for a moment, then laughed until he could barely catch his breath. Sadie couldn't help but join in, so much so that she snorted. They continued to cackle until they gasped for air and tears ran down their cheeks.

The sound of horse hooves clip-clopping and buggy

wheels rumbling into the parking lot caught Sadie's attention as her sides ached from all of the laughter. She craned her neck and peered through the downpour to get a better look at the approaching buggy. "There's Rhoda." Sadie motioned with a quick head movement, recognizing Rhoda's horse by the distinctive white heart-shaped patch on the muzzle. Pretty, red-haired Rhoda guided her horse up to the hitching rail beside Isaac's rig, then stared into the neighboring buggy with a visibly perplexed smile.

Sadie guffawed and waved at her friend. "One second," she called over the roar of the rain as she reached for her purse. She moved to bid farewell to Isaac but her heart caught in her throat when she turned to see him gazing intently at her. Isaac's chocolate-brown eyes had brightened significantly in just a few minutes and a warm smile decorated his chiseled face. Heat crept up the back of Sadie's neck and spread to her cheeks. Refusing to give in to excitement, she cleared her throat and returned a friendly smile. "*Denki* for letting me sit with you," she chirped. Then, in one swift motion, Sadie bounced from Isaac's buggy into Rhoda's, doing her best to ignore Rhoda's inquisitive glance.

"Who is your friend?" Rhoda questioned just above a whisper as she guided the horse away from the hitching post.

"His name is Isaac, and he and his mother just moved here from Indiana." Sadie tried to reply casually but her voice was trembling. She cleared her throat and sat taller. "He seems like a nice fellow."

"*Jah*, and handsome too." Rhoda wiggled her auburn eyebrows. "Seems like you two are already friends."

"I think a friend is just what he needs right now," Sadie responded as she settled back into her seat, rejecting Rhoda's gentle teasing.

"If it's a friend that he needs, he couldn't have found a better one," Rhoda complimented Sadie. "Seems like a perfect match."

Sadie scoffed and, about to respond with a witty joke, heard a male voice shout, "Hey, wait!"

Rhoda halted the horse and Sadie spun around in the direction of the voice. She was tickled to see Isaac's hat-absent head sticking out of his buggy. "You didn't tell me your name," he hollered.

Sadie chuckled as she watched the rain soak Isaac's mousy-blond hair, though he seemed unfazed. "Sadie Stolzfus," she called back, hoping he'd be able to make out what she'd said.

Isaac nodded, his bright, wide smile a brilliant sight amongst the dreary surroundings. "Nice to meet you, Sadie! Hope to see you around!"

"Me too," Sadie replied quietly, more to herself than anyone else.

When he returned to his new, albeit temporary, home, Isaac worked quickly to unhitch his aunt's horse, then made sure that the animal had a long, well-deserved drink. After that, he entered Aunt Miriam's house through the back door, deeply inhaling the delicious aroma of the supper she was whipping up. Hurrying upstairs, he quickly changed out of his rain-soaked clothes and donned dry attire.

Aenti Mim's house seemed far too large for a single older woman, with more spare rooms than anyone could possibly need. When he and his *mamm* had moved in yesterday, Mim had offered her sister the first choice of the available bedrooms, to which she had responded with a shrug. Isaac had hoped that his mother would take the front bedroom, with its many windows, since the extra sunlight would surely help her depressive, withdrawn state. Instead, she'd silently gravitated to the smallest, windowless, cavelike bedroom. But in a way, Isaac couldn't blame her for wanting to hide away from the world.

After the unexpected death of his childhood sweetheart, Isaac's world had promptly shattered. Rebecca King—the only woman he had ever loved and had planned to marry—had tragically passed away in a horrific accident, and Isaac refused to entertain the possibility that he could find love again in his lifetime. The way he saw it, a person only got a single shot at finding their soul mate, and his had been stolen from him far too soon.

After nearly two years of mourning, Isaac had accepted his fate as a permanent bachelor. If he couldn't build a life with Rebecca, he wouldn't build a life with any woman. Instead of worrying about himself, nearly all of his attention was now focused instead on his traumatized mother, who had become mute after witnessing the accident that had taken Rebecca's life. *If* Mamm *can recover, that is the best we can hope for.*

"But now is a time to focus on the future," Isaac declared aloud to himself as the encouraging effect of his encounter with Sadie continued to elevate his spirits. Even if his life was meant to be lived without love, nothing was stopping him from having a positive outlook on the rest of his life.

After tromping down the stairs, Isaac was glad to see Aunt Mim busily cooking up a storm and that his mother, Ruth, was seated at the table. With a warm smile on her face, Mim looked up from stirring the pot she stood over. "Just in time for dinner," she chirped. "How do you like your potatoes?"

"I like 'em mashed, if it's not a bother?" Isaac requested, already knowing that he would enjoy life with jolly Aunt Mim.

"*Gut*, because that's what I've already made!" Mim winked at him, then reached into the cupboard for three plates. "There's a kettle on the stove that your *mamm* just put on for tea. Should be ready any minute now."

"*Denki, Mamm.*" Isaac sincerely smiled, wishing his mother could comprehend just how thankful he was to see her taking this small step toward normalcy. She didn't answer, of course, but it was enough to see her making an effort. Maybe the change of scenery was already starting to help!

Isaac retrieved three mugs from the cupboard and joined his mother at the table. *Mamm* continued to stare blankly, her previously vibrant blue eyes now turned gray, focused on nothing in particular. Filled with pity at the sight of her, Isaac snapped to attention when the kettle began to whistle and dashed to retrieve it.

"I was thinking we should take our plates out to the front porch and eat outside tonight," Mim declared as she shoveled heaps of buttered noodles onto each plate.

Isaac chuckled at the comically large portions Mim had prepared but then stiffened at her suggestion. "But it's raining, *aentie*."

"The porch is covered and it's not blowing sideways like it was earlier," Mim countered as she handed Isaac three tea bags.

Isaac cringed at the suggestion. Rainy days were more difficult than most for him, and he noticed his mother seemed to share that sentiment. Going outside to hear the splashing of raindrops might stir up something that was best forgotten. "I think it'd be better to eat inside," Isaac quietly disagreed, putting a tea bag in each mug and then filling each cup with the scalding water.

"Oh, pfft!" Mim exclaimed, lifting all three plates at once like a seasoned waitress. "Fresh air is good for the lungs, even if it's a little damp. What do you say, *schwester*?"

Isaac waited for a reaction from his mother, feeling every muscle in his body tense with anxiety. Would she have an emotional outburst at the thought of going outdoors in this weather? To his surprise and relief, *Mamm* shrugged in response.

"What are we waiting for? Let's gobble this up before it gets cold," Mim triumphantly declared, pushing the screen door open with her backside. Wordlessly, *Mamm* gathered up the three steaming mugs and gingerly followed her sister out to the covered porch.

Astonished by Mim's convincing nature, Isaac

shrugged and headed to the porch as well. He took a seat in the chair next to his mother's, then stared down at his overflowing plate of roasted chicken, mashed potatoes, buttered noodles, carrots and coleslaw. Amish meals were known for lacking in nothing, but it had been quite some time since Isaac had enjoyed such a bountiful feast. With only his younger sisters doing the cooking at home recently, his meals had been disappointing compared to what Mim served up.

"You've outdone yourself, *aentie*," Isaac gushed, grabbing his fork eagerly.

Mim chortled. "With you two here to keep me company, there's no excuse for me to have my usual simple salad or bowl of cereal." Mim sipped her tea and glanced at Ruth with a twinkle in her eye. "Isaac, did you know that when your mother was about four years old, she tried to make her own bowl of cereal? Instead, she spilled an entire gallon of milk all over the kitchen floor and then pulled the area rug over the spill to hide the mess."

Isaac nearly choked on a mouthful of chicken. "Did anyone notice?"

"Not until a few days later when the room began to smell dreadful," Mim blurted, nearly unable to finish her sentence. "Our *mamm* didn't even try to clean the little rug. She took it outside and set it on fire!" Mim dabbed at the corners of her eyes while she continued to laugh.

Isaac joined Mim's rowdy laughter until his sides ached. When he composed himself, he took another bite of his dinner and asked, "Did you really do that,

Mamm?" No answer. Isaac wondered if she thought they were laughing at her, even though it was all in good fun. He glanced at her to see she was looking down at her plate, though she hadn't yet touched her food. "Aren't you gonna eat?" he questioned, hoping to urge her along. "It's awful tasty." Still no response. Isaac cleared his throat, realizing that he should have known better than to expect an answer from his mute parent.

As he forked some carrots into his mouth, Isaac looked out to Mim's well-kept front yard. Never married, unlike her nine siblings, Mim had lived with her parents in this very house until they'd passed away. She'd then kept up the house and small stable of animals by herself, as well as worked numerous jobs throughout her life. Now in her late fifties, Mim enjoyed quilting and entertaining the local children, both Plain and *Englisch*. Nearly every day, small groups of children came to her home to listen to her stories and eat her freshly baked cookies. Isaac admired his aunt and the life she had made for herself. He wondered if his future would be similar to hers, at least in the choice to live as a single person.

Mim must have seen him squinting through the rain and past the yard, across the quiet lane and to the fields of soybeans, corn and alfalfa that stretched farther than eyes could see. "How's Bird-in-Hand treating you so far?" she questioned, probably sensing that a change in subject was badly needed.

"*Ach*, it's beautiful," Isaac quickly replied, "though the tourists seem much more plentiful here than back home. Once you get to the back roads, it's more peaceful. You sure do live in a nice spot."

Mim nodded. "I wish your *daed* would move his woodworking business from Shipshewana, Indiana, to Lancaster County. The Lord has granted him success, but he'd have even more business here since the tourists always want to get their hands on anything that's Amish-made."

Isaac nodded as he scraped his fork against his plate, gathering up every last morsel of food. "Might be something for him to consider. I'll mention that in the letter I'm planning to send him."

Mim clapped her hands and the apples of her cheeks turned a cute rosy hue. "Wouldn't it be nice to have my whole family back in Lancaster again! I'm getting old, and I wanna spend as much time as I can with each one of you."

Isaac snorted and rolled his eyes. "You're not the least bit old, Mim, but I know what you mean. Life can change in an instant and it's best to spend as much time as you can with those you love."

Suddenly there was a clatter of a plate and utensils as *Mamm* shoved her untouched meal onto the small, wicker side table. Without a word, she rose from her seat, opened the screen door and retreated into the house.

Isaac sighed heavily and placed his hand to his head. "I shouldn't have said that."

Placing her empty plate next to her sister's untouched dish, Mim stood and then lowered herself into the empty chair next to her nephew. "It's all right. She knows you didn't mean anything by it. And I can see that she isn't the only one with a broken heart."

Isaac groaned. "I just wish I knew of something, anything, that could ease her suffering," he responded, ignoring Mim's comment about the state of his own grief. "I wish there was something that could bring a smile to her face, even if only for a moment!" He was startled when a brief image of Sadie Stolzfus flashed through his mind's eye.

"That's something that might be best left in *Gott*'s hands," Mim softly answered, briefly placing a hand on his shoulder.

Isaac ran his fingers through his thick, dirty-blond hair, still damp from the rain. "Well then, I sure wish He would hurry up."

Mim laughed again and Isaac couldn't help but smile. "Don't rush *Gott*'s timing, or you might just miss the little blessings He's planted for you along the way." Mim took his empty plate, placed it on top of hers, then picked up his mother's full dish in her other hand. She stood. "And besides, one of those blessings might be a nice girl."

Isaac resisted the urge to roll his eyes. He thought he'd escaped pestering from his father, friends and sisters to find himself a new girlfriend. Now, even here in Bird-in-Hand, it seemed like Mim would start pushing him to find a new love, and that was something that he was determined to avoid. When Isaac didn't respond, Mim shrugged and carried the dinner plates back inside the house.

As Isaac downed the last of his tea, he mulled over

Mim's proverb. Another image of pretty, spirited Sadie popped into his mind. He smirked at the memory of the ridiculous face she had made to get him laughing when he'd started to feel down. *Who'd have thought that a complete stranger could turn my day around?* Isaac mused, wondering if his unexpected introduction to Sadie had been orchestrated by *Gott* Himself.

Chapter Two

Sadie perched high in the branches of her favorite maple tree, which grew near the peak of her father's farm. From her seat in the branches, she took in a sea of *Gott*'s colorful creation before her. Whitewashed Amish and red *Englisch* barns dotted the landscape like freckles. Fields of alfalfa, tobacco, corn and soybeans danced together in a patchwork quilt of natural colors. After yesterday's stormy weather, the early August sun had no clouds to compete against. A calm breeze whispered through the leaves of the tree as Sadie inhaled the sweet summery scent of fresh-cut grass.

This is where I belong, Sadie reflected. It wasn't that she minded helping her mother and sister cook and clean. Traditional tasks of sewing, quilting and canning also were boring, but not a bother. Yet Sadie wasn't truly alive unless she could be outdoors, breathing in fresh air, marveling at the fireflies that sparkled at dusk, and watching her sunflowers grow into golden blossoms that sometimes soared feet above her head.

Swinging her legs, which hung over the mighty branch on which she sat, Sadie noticed a bluebird perched a few branches over. The bird hopped toward her, chirping a musical greeting. Sadie gently welcomed the blue-feathered critter, whistling to catch the bird's attention. "Hello, little friend."

"Hello?"

Sadie nearly fell out of the tree in surprise. She'd thought she was alone, except for her feathered companion, and surely the bird hadn't spoken to her. Grabbing the branch to steady herself, she leaned to her left and then to her right in an attempt to see through the foliage. When she found an opening large enough to see out of, she spied her twin, Moses, looking over his shoulder. He seemed to be just as startled as she had been. "Mose!" She called out to catch her brother's attention, using the nickname the entire Amish community had bestowed upon him at birth.

"Who's there?" Mose asked, pulling his dark eyebrows together while continuing to search his surroundings.

"It's Sadie!"

"Where are you?"

"I'm up here! In the tree!"

Mose scurried to the wide trunk of the tree and tipped his head in puzzlement. "I've been looking for you for over a half hour now," he shouted up, shielding his eyes from the sunlight that sprinkled through the leaves.

"Well, here I am," Sadie called back. If anyone but Mose had found her up a tree, a small flame of embarrassment would have burned in her chest. It was most unladylike, if not bizarre, for a grown woman to be climbing in a tree like a squirrel. While she assumed others frowned upon her spontaneous behavior, there was no need to tame her wildfire spirit around Mose. Maybe it was because they shared that special bond of being twins. Sadie called to her brother, "Just a second! I'll be right down."

"No, you stay there. I'll come up." Mose took hold of the lowest branch, pressed his boot against the tree trunk and propelled himself upward. Sadie tried to stifle her laughter. The feats of her tall, lanky brother twisting and scaling his way through the thick foliage was something to watch.

Mose wheezed as he lowered himself beside Sadie on the branch. "That was quite an obstacle course." He took his straw hat off and fanned his face. "At least you picked a strong branch to sit on. Don't want either of us to go tumbling to the ground."

Sadie nodded in agreement. "What brings you all the way up this tree?"

As if he was nervous, Mose plucked a leaf from the tree, then twirled its stem between his fingers. "What are you doing up here?" he asked, avoiding his sister's question.

"Just admiring the Lord's handiwork." Sadie gestured toward the marvelous vantage point she had found. "To tell you the truth, I've probably been up here too long. I'm sure *Mamm* is wondering where I am right about now," she admitted without a hint of shame. She sighed at the thought of her chores, filling her lungs with the pleasant, rural air. "If I didn't have any work, I'd probably stay up here all day."

"Well, you certainly picked a *gut*, if not challenging, place to observe all of creation from." Mose smiled, putting his hat back on and gazing into the distance where the cornstalk-covered hills met the periwinkle afternoon sky. He suddenly cleared his throat. "Today when *Daed* and I were hitching up the mules to go rake the hay, he asked if you were gonna attend the singing over at the Grabers' place next Sunday night."

Sadie raised her eyebrows at Mose's mention of their father's question. "I normally attend every singing, and you know that."

Mose stared at the leaf he was holding, then released it. He watched it float to the ground before speaking again. "*Jah*, I guess so."

Mose's obvious hesitation to explain things further ruined the peaceful atmosphere. He drummed his fingers on their branch seat as if he couldn't sit still. Laid-back Mose was never one to be fidgety, and for him to bring up a conversation he'd had with their father was enough to cause concern. Sadie leaned toward her twin. "I may enjoy sitting like a bird in this tree, but I know you're just itching to get your big feet back on the ground."

Mose grimaced at her words.

"Why did *Daed* ask if I was going to the singing?"

Her twin heaved a heavy sigh and tossed his dark, shaggy brunette hair out of his eyes. "To be truthful, I think he's a bit worried about you."

Sadie recoiled. "What does he have to worry about?"

"*Ach*, Sadie, you sure are making this awful difficult." Mose looked away from her for a moment. "I think our *daed* is concerned for you because he hasn't yet heard any rumors about you, if you catch my drift."

"A *daed* who doesn't hear rumors about his *dochder* should be a proud father," Sadie replied, irked at the direction that their conversation had taken.

"Now hold on, will you? What I'm saying…well, you're twenty-one years old now and—"

"And so are you," Sadie interrupted, wanting to put an end to the discussion before it went any further.

"Could you be serious for just a minute?" Mose pleaded with a grumble. "*Daed* hasn't heard any rumors about who you might be courting." Mose clenched his teeth and stared at her as if bracing for the impact of her response.

Sadie narrowed her eyes, aggravated that her father had brought up her nonexistent love life to Mose. Why wouldn't her father have just spoken directly to her if he had something to say? Why on earth was he trying to meddle?

"Sadie…" Mose cautiously ventured, still anxiously waiting for a reply.

"*Daed* hasn't heard any talk through the grapevine because there isn't anything to talk about," Sadie retorted, crossing her arms over her chest.

"But you're twenty-one." Mose repeated his earlier statement, swatting away a fly that had joined them. "Most girls your age are fixing to get married or are at least being courted by a nice guy. He's just worried that—"

"He has absolutely nothing to worry about," Sadie interrupted again. "I joined the church when I was fifteen. I'm not out running around the world, doing things that a Plain girl has no business doing. Why isn't that enough for him?"

"Listen, Sadie," Mose interjected, "I didn't mean to upset you, and neither does our *daed*. He just doesn't want to see his *dochder* end up…alone."

"I know." Hot tears burned in the back of Sadie's eyes, but she refused to let them fall. "You can tell *Daed* he needn't worry. If I'm ever spoken for, I'm sure the gossip will get to him soon enough."

"I don't know if that will be enough, Sadie. I overheard him talking to *Mamm* while I was putting my work boots on after breakfast this morning." Mose grimaced, then looked away from her, his shoulders sagging. "They agreed that if you couldn't find yourself a beau by the first of October, they will find someone for you."

A sudden feeling of nausea quivered through Sadie. She knew that her parents were thinking of matchmaking, but never expected that she'd face an ultimatum so soon. October was only two months away, and Sadie had no romantic prospects on the horizon. Of course, her parents would never force her to marry someone, but life in their house would quickly become miserable for her if they started to meddle in her personal life. Sadie simply refused to marry, or even date a fellow, if there wasn't a legitimate connection. What was the point of sharing her life with someone who didn't make her heart soar like an eagle? The problem was that she knew there were no Amish bachelors in her community who seemed to have an interest in her due to her fiery spirit and quirky nature, and she was unwilling to change who *Gott* created her to be.

"Sadie? Are you all right?"

Sadie glanced at her brother. "Of course I'm not all right. How would you feel if you were being forced to court someone just for the sake of courting?" She planted her hands on her hips, her tone sounding almost like a snake's angry hiss. "You're twenty-one and single too. Why aren't *Mamm* and *Daed* forcing this on you as well?"

Mose chewed on his bottom lip. "I understand how you feel, and I agree that you shouldn't date someone just for the sake of courting." He let out a small chuckle but then covered it up with an obviously fake cough. "I suppose it won't hurt to let the cat out of the bag now. I've been letter-writing with Rhoda Zook, and I've asked to give her a ride home in my courting buggy after the Grabers' singing." Mose's mouth contorted oddly as he stifled a grin.

Sadie looked away from her brother to hide her reaction. In her heart, she was overjoyed to hear that her twin brother and dearest friend might be starting a relationship. Still, the sting of the realization that she was the last single girl among her friend group bit at her soul like a horsefly that couldn't be swatted away. Putting on her bravest face, she took several breaths before replying to her brother's news. "That's *wunderbar*, Mose. Rhoda is a really nice *maedel*, and I know for a fact that she's had her eye on you for quite some time."

Mose's pathetically hidden smile burst into a full-on grin before he seemingly regained control of his facial expression. "*Denki*, but what about you? Will you at least pray that a suitable fellow will make his presence known? Finding love will make you happy, and will keep *Mamm* and *Daed* at bay."

Sadie sighed and tried to nod, but the movement was so slight that she wasn't sure if her head had moved at all. "*Jah*, I will," she finally agreed, knowing that prayer never hurt anyone.

Mose gave her a relieved, crooked smile. "That's all I needed to hear. I better get back to work." He leaned forward, looking down at the ground far below, then shivered. "How does one get down from here?"

Sadie chuckled against the sadness that threatened to eat her alive. "Very carefully."

Clearly unamused by her less than helpful reply, Mose rolled his eyes, then gingerly crept down the tree, staying near the sturdy trunk.

Once her brother was out of earshot, Sadie let go of the tears she had been holding back. It wasn't that she didn't want a beau, or to be married with a house full of children to love. Throughout her teenage years, she'd experienced a handful of schoolgirl crushes on her male peers, though they'd all turned out to be unrequited. As a grown woman, her prospects of finding love were even grimmer. What conservative Amish fellow would want a woman who refused to let her childlike delight for life be tamed?

"Is there a man out there who would love me for who

I am, lively soul and all?" Sadie wondered out loud. "Oh, Lord, if there is such a man, send him to me!"

After a day or two of settling into his new home, Isaac had insisted on caring for Mim's small barn of animals, which included her horse and two Holstein cows. Isaac enjoyed spending time with the peaceful animals and making small repairs to the old barn, but now he was focusing on the task of morning milking.

Isaac was nearly knocked to his feet when the more ornery of the two cows gave him a good bump. Losing his balance, he swayed unsteadily. "Stubborn," he muttered under his breath. When Isaac calmly inched closer to the cow to begin milking, the animal stepped forward, placing her hoof on top of his foot.

"Yow!" Isaac jumped around on one leg, holding the sore foot with both hands. "You big, dumb thing!"

He heard a woman suddenly burst into laughter. He spun around and was surprised to see a thin, dark-haired young woman entering the barn. She held a basket filled to the brim with treats, and the delicious aroma of baked goods caused Isaac to forget about his throbbing foot.

"I'm so sorry," the woman said between giggles, her face flushed with laughter. "That was a funny little dance you just did." She covered her mouth with her slender hand and failed to suppress another outburst.

Isaac couldn't help but grin when he replayed the scene in his head. "I suppose it was." With the sleeve of his shirt, he wiped at some of the sweat that had beaded on his forehead. "What can I do for you today?"

"I just heard through the grapevine that we had new

neighbors who moved in with Miriam. My family runs a roadside stand and I wanted to bring you some of our best sellers as a welcome." The woman held out the basket that contained jars of homemade apple butter and peach jelly, two loaves of friendship bread, and a package of assorted cookies.

Accepting the basket, Isaac smiled in appreciation. "That's real kind of you. *Denki*, uh…"

"Nancy Beiler."

"Nancy." Isaac nodded his head. "I'm Isaac Hostettler."

"I know," she seemed unashamed to admit, though she turned a bright shade of pink.

An uneasy feeling settled in the pit of Isaac's stomach. Was that eagerness he saw in her eyes? Maybe she was lonely and looking to make a new friend. What if she was looking for something more?

A wave of panic crashed into Isaac's chest. No, that was an utterly ridiculous thought.

"Well, Isaac—" Nancy squeaked at the end of his name "—maybe I can make supper for you sometime." She pulled her arms behind her back and twisted in half circles without moving her feet.

Feeling uncomfortable yet not wanting to hurt the poor woman's feelings, Isaac kicked at some loose straw on the barn floor. "That's kind of you, but my *mamm*'s still getting settled in here. I want to make sure she's all right before I stray too far away from home."

"What about Miriam? Doesn't she care for her *schwester* when you can't be by her side?"

Isaac was taken aback, feeling suddenly defensive

of his family. "Sure she does, but Mim also looks after some children from time to time, and she has plenty of chores around the house. She can't be with *Mamm* all the time."

Nancy squinted at Isaac as if she wasn't sure that she believed him. He half expected her to invite his mother and aunt to dinner as well, just to be polite. Instead, she smiled pleasantly at him and shrugged in defeat. "Okay then, maybe another time." She glanced at the fresh manure that was just a few feet away and made a sour face. "I guess I'll leave you to your work. It was nice to meet you!" As quickly as she had appeared, Nancy turned on her heels and scurried away.

"Sure," Isaac muttered, wishing he could say the same. He watched as she dashed out of the barn, somehow knowing that this would not be his last strange encounter with Nancy Beiler.

Chapter Three

Later that week, Isaac eagerly approached the Stolzfus barn with a spring in his step. He would need a buggy horse of his own while residing in Bird-in-Hand, and Aunt Mim had recommended Mose Stolzfus as "the very best horse trader around these parts." Besides, having a horse of his own would certainly help him feel more at home in this new community.

Reaching the open barn doors, Isaac politely peered inside before entering. "Hello? Anybody home?"

"Just me and the animals," answered a lanky, dark-haired Amish man. He ran a currycomb through the chestnut coat of a horse that stood proudly beside him. With a welcoming grin, the man stepped away from the horse and extended his hand to Isaac. "Mose Stolzfus."

Isaac took Mose's hand, shaking it firmly. "Nice to meet you, Mose. I'm Isaac Hostettler. My aunt Mim said you'd be expecting me."

Mose nodded enthusiastically. "I sure was. I hear you're in the market for a driving horse."

"That's right. Can't be using my aunt's horse every time I need to go somewhere." Isaac reached out to pet the proud horse's shiny, impeccably groomed coat. "Mim said you're the best person to buy a horse from in Lancaster County."

Mose grinned at the compliment. "That's awful nice of her to say. I try to only buy the horses I would want for myself." He ran his fingers through the horse's ebony mane as if he was hunting for tangles. Clearly, he took excellent care of his animals. "I assume you're looking for someone who's a good trotter, and pretty agile as well?"

"I don't know what I'm looking for." Isaac chuckled as he rubbed the back of his neck. "I suppose I'll know the right horse when I see it, though."

Mose seemed to understand. "I'll be glad to show you each horse I have, and you can tell me if one strikes your fancy." He gestured toward the noble steed beside them. "This is Samson. He's a five-year-old, standard-bred gelding." As if Samson knew he was being critiqued, he stood just so, with his head high in the air. "He's an ex-racehorse who I bought off a trainer in the Poconos just a few weeks ago," Mose said. "Want to take him out for a run?"

Isaac squinted at the horse, and the horse glared back at him. "I better see who else you have first," Isaac declined.

Mose showed Isaac two similar horses he thought could also make a fine match. Still, Isaac hadn't met the right horse for him. When they approached the final stall, Isaac's face lit up like the night sky on the Fourth of July. "Who is this?" he asked, petting the horse's muzzle as it approached.

Mose's face contorted as if he was genuinely shocked by Isaac's interest in the animal. "That's just Shadow. To be up-front with you, he's not the fastest or spunkiest of the bunch." He pulled a sugar cube out of a nearby container and gave it to Shadow. "I wasn't going to bring him home, but my twin sister carried on until I did."

Isaac ran his hand over the horse's gray-and-white-spotted coat. "Is there something wrong with him?"

"Not at all," Mose answered with a prompt shake of his head. "He's as healthy as they come. He's just older and slower. I didn't think anyone would be interested in purchasing him, but Sadie insisted."

As if on cue, there was a commotion in the hayloft overhead. Both men looked up just in time to see Sadie leap from the open second story and grab hold of the old rope swing that hung from the ceiling. Isaac and Mose jumped back as she sailed past at a terrifying speed, her dress and the ties of her *kapp* flying in the breeze behind her.

The rope gradually slowed, but before it came to a complete halt, Sadie let go and landed with a thud on the dusty barn floor. "Sorry to interrupt," she apologized as she shook some loose hay off her apron.

"How could you not interrupt with an entrance like that?" Mose replied with a hearty laugh. "What in the world were you doing up there?" he questioned, still smiling at Sadie.

"Reading the Good Book," Sadie stated, pulling her well-used Bible out from beneath her arm. "*Mamm* has friends visiting and I wanted to give them their privacy." She glanced at Isaac and her face instantly brightened. "Hi, Isaac! Are you here to buy Shadow?"

Isaac's mouth still hung open in disbelief. What a tremendously unexpected surprise to see this lively girl again. "Hi, Sadie. I sure was considering it. I think we'd make a good match."

Sadie bounded up to the horse and wrapped her arms around its strong neck. "*Jah*, he's beautiful. His colorful coat makes him stand out from the rest of the brown buggy horses."

As if worried that Isaac might be swayed by Sadie's fond talk of the animal, Mose stepped forward. "Samson or one of the other two geldings would make for a better buggy horse. Shadow is more of a pet, I think."

Isaac studied Mose, then Sadie, then Shadow. Finally, he proclaimed, "There's something I like about Shadow, and I don't need the fastest horse money can buy. I'd like to take him out for a ride first, but I think I'd like to buy him from you."

Sadie squealed and embraced the horse again. "You hear that, Shadow? You're getting a new home!" Whipping back around, Sadie waltzed out of the barn just as quickly as she had appeared, calling "So long, Isaac" over her shoulder.

Isaac watched Sadie leave, astonished by the experience. He'd never known a grown woman to have such an enthusiastic outlook on the world around her, and it was downright refreshing.

Mose smirked and failed to smother a cackle. "You've met my twin sister before?"

"Just the other day, when we had that severe downpour," Isaac responded, still staring out the barn door, though Sadie was now long gone. "She's very, um…"

"Spirited." Mose finished the sentence when Isaac was at a loss for words. Isaac sheepishly nodded, wondering if he had stepped on any toes. Mose chuckled affectionately while picking up a bridle to put on Shadow. "I don't know of anyone as spirited as our Sadie. Living with her sure makes life more exciting."

Isaac agreed. The two finished hitching up the horse, then led the gentle animal to Mose's open courting buggy, which was resting just outside the barn door.

Once Shadow was fully hitched up to the carriage, Mose handed the reins to Isaac. "The young people from our district are having a singing next Sunday evening at Pete Graber's farm," Mose stated. "I hope you plan to attend."

Now seated in Mose's courting buggy, Isaac rubbed his knee, milling over the idea. It would be fun to socialize with the other Amish youth in Bird-in-Hand, but would it be fair to attend if he wasn't looking for a mate? "It's been a long time, years in fact, since I've attended a youth gathering," Isaac declared, trying to hide the sadness in his voice. "I don't know if I would fit in."

"Sure you would," Mose cautiously ventured as he leaned against his buggy. "Not having attended a singing in a while is the perfect reason to go and have yourself a *gut* time! Besides, Sadie and I will be there, so there'll be some friendly faces if you decide to join us. And you'll make lots of new friends."

"True," Isaac confessed, staring at Shadow as he

swatted away some pesky flies with his granite-colored tail. "Let me talk to Shadow about it while I take him out on the road. He's an old man, so he should have the wisdom of Solomon, *jah*?"

Mose snorted at Isaac's joke while Isaac guided Shadow down the long driveway. As he observed Shadow's gait and personality, his thoughts drifted back to Sadie and the second dramatic entrance she'd made into his life. There was something sweet and silly about her that could make anyone forget their troubles within minutes of meeting her. Maybe he needed a bit more of Sadie's enthusiasm for life.

Sadie closed the lid of her family's mailbox and sorted through the letters in her hand. She had been feeling a bit gloomy ever since Mose had clued her in on their parents' imminent plans to find her a mate, and she'd hoped that today's mail would have included a letter or two from one of her many Amish pen pals. An interesting letter would certainly lift her spirits, but she was disappointed to see that there was no mail for her. She wished something would happen to take her mind off her troubles as she headed back up the long, winding drive.

When she was about halfway to the house, she stopped to wave at Isaac as he passed by with Shadow. To her surprise, he pulled on the reins and brought Mose's courting buggy to a halt. Sadie put a hand to her forehead to shield her eyes from the sun. "Taking Shadow out for a test ride?"

Isaac nodded and adjusted his straw hat. "*Jah*, but it's

really only a formality. I'm gonna buy him from Mose once we get back from our ride."

"I'm glad to hear that Shadow will finally have a permanent home, but I sure will miss seeing him around here," Sadie confessed as she reached out to pet the dapple-gray.

"If you're not busy at the moment, you should come for a ride with us. It'll give you a chance to make one more memory with Shadow before I take him home," Isaac suggested, his handsome smile nearly outshining the intense August sun.

"Well, don't mind if I do!" Sadie bounced up into the rig and scooted next to Isaac on the driver's bench. A ride with her new friend through the rolling farmlands of Lancaster County would be the perfect medicine to soothe her spirit. Sadie stuffed the mail into her apron pocket as Isaac gently flicked the reins to get Shadow moving, and soon they were headed onto Stumptown Road.

A few minutes of comfortable silence passed between the pair as Sadie listened to the rhythmic clopping of Shadow's hooves. She closed her eyes for just a moment, deeply inhaling the sweet country air. The earthy scents of growing corn and fresh stream water invigorated her as the buggy traveled past Mill Creek. When she opened her eyes, she peeked over at Isaac, and she couldn't help but stare at the contented smile on his attractive face. There was something that felt natural about being in his presence, though they had only known each other a short time.

Isaac took his eyes off the road for just a second and glanced over at her. "Penny for your thoughts, Sadie."

Sadie felt her heart jump into her throat, realizing that she had been caught staring at him. She scrambled to come up with something to say other than admitting that she had been a bit mesmerized by his company. "I was wondering how your first week has been in Lancaster County. Are you enjoying it here?"

"*Ach*, very much so," Isaac replied as he yanked on the reins to guide Shadow down another road. "I do miss my *daed* and *schwesters*, but *Mamm* and I really needed a change of scenery. Plus, it's nice to spend some time with my Mim. I only met her once when I was a little *buwe* when she traveled to Indiana to visit us." He glanced again at Sadie with a crooked smile and a twinkle in his eye. "I met some real nice folks recently too." He winked at her and then turned his attention back to the country road before them.

So he enjoys my company as well, Sadie realized as she grinned at Isaac. She sat a little taller in her seat, enjoying the notion that Isaac seemed to appreciate her for who she was. She didn't need to dull her sparkle to feel accepted. "You should come to the singing that's gonna take place at the Graber farm next Sunday."

"Mose mentioned the singing earlier." Isaac let out a sigh. "I didn't want to go at first, but Mose also brought up the possibility of making some more friends, so I decided that I'll attend."

"Why didn't you want to go? Singings are always a good time."

Isaac's cute smile contorted into an awkward expression. As he brought the buggy to a halt at a stop sign, he seemed to be mulling over how he should reply to her question. "After the past two years I've had, I know I'll never go courting ever again."

Sadie took in Isaac's somber words. Not wanting to pry, Sadie nodded understandingly. "I'm real sorry to hear that, Isaac."

His shoulders sagged as he made a clicking sound to get the horse moving again. "*Denki.* I don't want to dwell on the past." He cleared his throat, perhaps to keep his emotions at bay. "Anyway, I'm not interested in finding love ever again, and that's really the point of the singings, *jah*?"

Filled with compassion for her new friend, Sadie quickly thought of a supportive response. "That's true, but you can still go just for some fellowship with the other young people. We will be glad to see you there."

"I know that I'll enjoy myself at the singing, but I just worry that the ladies will think that I'm looking to find someone to court." Even though it was a humid summer day, Sadie thought she saw Isaac shiver. "A *maedel* came to *Aentie* Mim's place a few days ago, and I got the distinct impression that she was on the hunt for a husband. I wouldn't want to lead her on."

"Sounds like you met Nancy Beiler," Sadie ventured.

"*Jah*, that was her!"

Isaac's confirmation caused Sadie to let out a belly laugh—that and the fact that Isaac's eyes had grown as large as dinner plates. Once her chortling ceased, she wiped the tears from her emerald eyes. "I understand your concern, but you can't let what others think dictate how you live your life." The melancholy that she'd felt earlier that day started to creep back up on her. "Folks make fun of me because I'd much rather climb a tree and marvel at all the Lord created for us instead of sewing a quilt. I'd rather be out in the meadow, watching a calf be born instead of baking a pie. It's why I'm still single."

She rubbed her forehead where she felt a headache coming. "A few weeks ago my *daed* told me that I should stop playing in the dirt and quit my part-time job at the greenhouse so I could focus on finding myself a husband. The other day I learned that my parents are planning to match me up with someone if I don't have a steady boyfriend by the first of October."

Isaac shook his head and moved his shoulders in a quick shrug. "That's *baremlich*, Sadie. You shouldn't conform to who someone else wants you to be. I think it's nice that you so thoroughly enjoy the world that the Lord created for us. The right man will come along, and he will love you for the sweet *maedel* that I know you are."

A rush of heat passed over Sadie's cheeks. She hadn't expected such a compliment from Isaac. Her heart stirred, knowing that Isaac seemed like more than a friend; they were kindred spirits. "*Jah*, well, unless you want to court me, it looks like I'll be subject to my parents' meddling come harvesttime." Sadie's heart dropped when the words left her lips, and her hand flew to her chest to still its frenzied beating. "Isaac, I'm so sorry. I didn't mean to imply…"

"Actually—" Isaac cut her off "—that would solve

some problems for both of us." He waved at the driver of a passing horse and buggy, then returned his free hand to the reins. "I mean, I need an excuse not to date Nancy Beiler—or anyone, for that matter. You need yourself a beau to stop your *mamm* and *daed* from trying to fix you up with someone against your will."

Sadie's mouth fell open, shocked that he would actually consider faking a courtship. "You're serious about this?"

"Well, I don't want to deceive folks." He grinned at her sheepishly. "But desperate times call for desperate measures, I suppose."

"But how…what…?"

"Look, there's a little restaurant up ahead. Let's stop for lunch and we can figure out the details there." Isaac chuckled, then wiggled his eyebrows at Sadie. "We can consider it our first date."

"*Jah*, that sounds good," Sadie agreed. A strange mixture of relief and disappointment floated around her mind. Isaac did make some good points about the mutual benefits of feigning a courtship, but she'd always imagined that her first date would involve some sort of a love connection. Ignoring the nagging reminder that she was destined to become a spinster, she decided to enjoy her date with Isaac. He was a kind person who didn't pressure her to be someone she wasn't, and that was enough to make her smile.

Chapter Four

When Isaac and Sadie entered the quaint countryside diner, they were immediately greeted by the Mennonite hostess, who led them to their table. Once they slid into opposite sides of the booth, they were each handed a sizeable menu to look over. Isaac perused the menu but was distracted when Sadie suddenly started quietly humming a hymn. He glanced up at her, enjoying the simple melody as she read the menu, perhaps not even realizing that she was singing.

He hoped faking a courtship was truly the best thing for both of them. Isaac worried as he continued to study Sadie. There was a possibility that maintaining a feigned relationship could become complicated. It was a wonder to him that she wasn't spoken for. With her golden hair and grass-green eyes, she was a perfect example of natural beauty. It was a shame that the young men in this community didn't appreciate her unusually enthusiastic nature. So what if she was a bit childlike in her enjoyment of the truly simple things in life? Would the young men rather date a boring girl who had nothing special about her?

If his heart didn't already belong to Rebecca, he might be interested in properly courting Sadie himself. Startled by the thought, Isaac shoved it to the back of his mind. He'd been blessed to experience true love once, and that was enough for him. He refused to put his heart on the line again.

Soon a middle-aged *Englisch* waitress approached the table to take their orders. Sadie asked for a lemonade, a BLT sandwich and a side of applesauce. When the waitress turned to Isaac, he realized that he'd been too busy watching Sadie to decide on what to order. "I'll have the same," he said, handing both menus to the waitress before she scurried back to the kitchen.

"I don't know about you, but I'm mighty hungry. If our food doesn't come soon, I might just eat this place mat," Isaac joked, resting his folded hands on the paper place mat in front of him.

Sadie chuckled, then leaned forward, her face growing more serious than Isaac had ever seen it. "I don't think I can eat a single thing until we iron out the details of this courtship." The waitress returned to the table, dropped off their beverages and two straws, then hustled away once more. Once the woman was out of earshot, Sadie spoke again. "Are you absolutely certain you want to be my beau, Isaac?" Her eyes shone as if she was worried that he might decide to back out of their deal.

"*Jah*, I think that is what's best for both of us," Isaac replied without hesitation.

"All right, for how long?"

Isaac was a bit stunned by Sadie's candid but legitimate question. However, he appreciated her direct nature. "How about we court for a year?"

Sadie shook her head. "I think that's too long. Surely there will come a day when some girl catches your attention, and you may want to be free to court her."

Isaac glanced out the window and frowned, noticing some dark, heavy-looking clouds approaching. "That won't happen."

"Well, you never know."

"Trust me, it won't." Isaac's response came out harsher than he'd intended. And it caused Sadie to shrink back in her seat. He sighed, glancing again at the rain clouds approaching in the distance. "If I were to meet a girl who could teach me to love the rain, I'll know she's the one."

Sadie looked at him in obvious confusion, her lips parting slightly as she studied him. Isaac waited in painful suspense, dreading the required explanation that would follow such an unusual statement. Much to his relief, Sadie didn't pry and instead asked, "How about six months? That will get me far past my parents' October deadline, and that should also be long enough for Nancy to become interested in the next unsuspecting young man."

Isaac grinned at Sadie's colorful description. "Six months it is." He offered his hand to Sadie so they could shake on their agreement. The handshake lasted a bit longer than expected, and Isaac was surprised when neither one of them made the first move to pull their hand away.

However, the handshake abruptly ended when the waitress returned with their sandwiches and applesauce. "Now that that's settled, I'd like to hear more about your job at the greenhouse."

Sadie's face brightened at the mention of her workplace. "I've worked there two or three days a week for the past six years. I just adore all of the different flowers and plants." She took a bite of her sandwich, then went on. "I get to learn a lot about all of the different varieties of plants and how to care for them. Each one is so unique." She looked up from her plate and smiled at Isaac. "*Gott*'s ever so creative, *jah*?"

Isaac bobbed his head in agreement. Sadie's passion for gardening was contagious, and it stirred up an idea in Isaac. "You'll have to show me around the greenhouse someday. Mim has some empty flower beds that could sure use some color."

"That's a *gut* idea," Sadie replied as she used her napkin to wipe her face. "What did you do for work back in Indiana?"

"My *daed* owns a woodworking shop, and I've worked alongside him for as long as I can remember. We make a lot of furniture and some decorations that the tourists really enjoy, but I'm much more keen on farming. I hope to run my own dairy farm someday," Isaac confessed before taking the last bite of his sandwich.

"There's just something special about tending to the Lord's creation, *jah*?"

Sadie's statement warmed Isaac's heart. She understood his love for being outdoors, getting his hands dirty and caring for everything the Lord had created. "*Jah*, there sure is."

As they finished their meal, Isaac couldn't help but notice that he felt more chipper than he had in years. He thoroughly enjoyed Sadie's company, and he was honored to be her beau, even though it was only for a short while.

Sadie spent the rest of the day with some extra pep in her step. Her surprise outing with Isaac had been the highlight of her morning, and she replayed memories of their conversations in her mind as she spent her afternoon pulling weeds in her vegetable garden, helping her father and Mose with the evening milking chores, and assisting her mother with preparing dinner. She couldn't recall ever having such lively, interesting discussions with anyone before, and she looked forward to her next outing with Isaac, which would be the upcoming singing at the Graber farm.

After the supper dishes were washed and put away, Sadie decided to enjoy the rest of the evening by sitting on the porch swing and doing some journaling. With her journal and pen in hand, she padded across the wrap-around covered porch and took a seat on one of the swings. Before she opened her journal, she took in the familiar beauty that surrounded her family's farm. Her flower beds were fit to burst with vibrant reds, pinks and golds that paired nicely with the cool purplish hue of the dusk sky. Fireflies twinkled like glitter throughout the backyard, and an occasional contented moo could be heard from the pasture where the cows had been set free to graze. Cool evening air filled and refreshed her lungs just as her time spent with Isaac had been a balm to her soul. It had been a marvelous day, and Sadie sent up a quick prayer of thanks for the many blessings that she had received.

Opening her journal to a fresh page, Sadie began to neatly document the day's events. She had only been writing for a few minutes when the sound of familiar footsteps clomped up the porch stairs. She looked up to see Mose and patted the empty spot beside her on the seat. "Care to swing with me a spell?"

"I would, but I'm actually planning to turn in early tonight. I've got a driver coming to pick me up at four thirty tomorrow morning. He's gonna take me to Ohio to buy some horses." He leaned against the porch railing and crossed his arms at his chest. "Speaking of horses, I sold Shadow to that Isaac fellow."

"That's *wunderbar*," Sadie replied, unable to hide a growing smile. "I told you the right person would think he was the perfect horse for them."

"*Jah*, sure did." Mose glanced at one of the barn cats that had wandered onto the porch. The black-and-white feline walked up to him and rubbed against his leg. "So, how did your date go with Isaac?" Mose asked as he reached down to pet the friendly cat.

Sadie's mouth fell open. "H-how did you know?"

"I was standing outside the barn, giving one of the horses a bath, when I saw him returning from his ride with Shadow." A coy smile spread across Mose's face, which reminded Sadie of a cat that had just caught a mouse. "I saw him drop you off at the house before bringing Shadow and my rig back to the barn. He mentioned that you and he had met earlier this week, and I thought maybe he'd asked to take you out and seized the opportunity today."

Before Sadie could respond, the screen door squeaked open and their parents stepped outside. Mose issued Sadie a playfully knowing look, made some small talk with their parents, then retreated into the house.

"Sadie, your *mamm* and I need to have a talk with you about something important," announced her father, Amos, as he took a seat on the top porch step. "Got a minute to spare for your old *daed* and *mamm*?"

"Of course, I always do," Sadie answered with a small smile that hopefully hid her apprehension. She placed her journal and pen on the ground, then picked up the cat Mose had been petting.

Sadie's mother, Anna, took a seat next to her daughter on the swing. "Sadie, your *daed* and I noticed that sometimes it seems like you're lonely." The middle-aged woman reached out to pet the cat nestled into her daughter's lap, then shot a look of sympathy at her offspring.

"We want you to be a happy *maedel* who lives a fulfilling life," her father added, his concern for her shining like stars in his green eyes, which Sadie had inherited from him.

"I'm already fulfilled," Sadie replied just above a whisper, though she knew that this was only partially true. She longed to fall in love, but at the same time, she wasn't willing to tame her fiery spirit for any man, and she was certain that this was what her parents were getting at. "I have a job at the greenhouse that I love, and every day I get to spend time outdoors. What more could I ask for?"

"*Jah*, but there is more to life than planting flowers and climbing trees," retorted her mother. Though she was nearing fifty years of age, Anna normally didn't look a day over forty. However, the concern etched across her pretty face aged her unusually. "*Daed* and I think it's far past time for you to start courting. If you want to raise a family of your own, you'll need to find a suitable husband soon."

"That's why *Mamm* and I have decided to set you up with one of our friend's unmarried sons if you don't find yourself a beau by October first," Amos stated matter-of-factly, as if this was a perfectly reasonable solution.

Sadie bit her tongue. Though she knew that her parents had her best interests in mind, she couldn't bring herself to look at either of them. "Actually, I have met someone. I went on a lunch date with a nice man today."

Anna and Amos exchanged surprised glances. "Who is this man?" Amos asked, rising from his seat on the steps.

"His name is Isaac Hostettler. He and his *mamm* just moved here from Indiana, and they are living with his aunt, Miriam Fisher." Sadie looked up from petting the cat that had fallen asleep on her lap. "You'll get to meet them at the next church gathering, I'm sure."

Her mother's stunned expression quickly morphed into one of cautious relief. "Is he a baptized member of the Amish church?"

"*Jah*, he is," Sadie confirmed, having gleaned this

information during her lunch date with Isaac. "You can ask Mose about him too. He sold Shadow to Isaac earlier today."

"Well, this is real *gut* news, Sadie! Real *gut* indeed," *Daed* congratulated her with a bit of a chuckle. "I knew there was hope for you."

After a few more minutes of conversation, Sadie's parents headed back indoors, leaving her alone with her thoughts. A mix of conflicting emotions swirled together within Sadie as she gingerly lifted the sleeping cat from her lap and snuggled the animal like a teddy bear. She had managed to avoid her parents' meddling in her personal life, but it was a bittersweet mix of relief and disappointment.

Isaac was a kind, genuine, caring man, but Sadie had always imagined being in love when the day finally came that she would tell her parents about her first courtship. Instead, she was a girlfriend in name only. No feelings were involved, except for the butterflies that Isaac gave her whenever he stared into her eyes or smiled at her like she was a field full of wildflowers.

Lord, Sadie fervently prayed, *bless the time that Isaac and I spend together. Heal Isaac's broken heart, and send the right man to love me.*

Chapter Five

On the following Sunday afternoon, Isaac pulled his newly purchased buggy into the Graber family's driveway, surprised by the number of carriages already parked in the field. He knew he'd been running a few minutes late, but had never expected to see that the volleyball game had already begun.

Shrugging off his late arrival, Isaac stepped out of his buggy and hurried to unhitch Shadow. Then he led the horse to the pasture, releasing the dapple-gray to graze freely. Squatting next to the front right wheel of his rig, he reached up to the buggy's seat and pulled down a blue ribbon that Mim had given him. "Better take this along," she'd suggested when she'd offered the ribbon to him. "You can use this as a marker to tell your buggy apart from the others." Smiling at the reminder of Mim's cleverness, Isaac tied the ribbon on one of the front wheel's wooden spokes. Then he headed toward the gathering.

Isaac's attention was instantly drawn to the volleyball net set up in the middle of the neighboring field. This game seemed to be girls against boys. The young women had gathered on one side of the net, giggling and whispering to each other. The young men stood on the other side, eagerly discussing their game plan. A large folding table with a variety of snacks and beverages had been set up under an enormous oak tree and was drawing a sizeable crowd. Feeling his stomach rumble, Isaac decided that he required something to munch on.

He scanned the trays of baked goods and finally settled on a pumpkin whoopie pie. Turning from the table, he faced the volleyball game, snack in hand. He felt a bit overwhelmed as he watched the group of his peers. There were plenty of young Amish folks milling about the Grabers' fields and backyard. With such a large number of unfamiliar faces surrounding him, Isaac felt like an outsider. Plagued with sudden shyness, he continued to stand near the refreshment table, eating and scanning for a familiar face.

A burst of laughter broke out near the volleyball game. One of the chuckling female voices was considerably louder and more contagious than the others. Recognizing Sadie's voice immediately, Isaac quickly located her among the female players. Her bright smile outshone those around her. As she ran after the volleyball, occasionally scoring a point for her team, her energy was evident. It was obvious that the other young ladies enjoyed Sadie's company, and she frequently encouraged those around her with pats on the back and high fives.

Isaac continued to marvel at Sadie's every move. It

wasn't just her friendly and outgoing nature that was special. Her cute button nose and warm green eyes also made her the most attractive woman at the gathering. Once again, Isaac found himself baffled by Sadie's singleness. The other young men must be out of their minds not to take notice of such a passionate, albeit unusual, lovely lady.

"There you are, Isaac! I've been looking for you!" It was Nancy Beiler, heading right for him. Her hurried pace indicated that she was on a mission, and Isaac felt certain that he was the prize.

"Hello, Nancy," Isaac greeted her as she stepped up to him, nearly invading his personal space. "Nice day for a get-together, *jah*?"

"Indeed it is," Nancy replied as she wrung her hands together. "I'm glad to see you're here today. I was worried that you wouldn't come."

Isaac peered over Nancy's shoulder so he could continue watching Sadie. He found her to be much more interesting than Nancy Beiler, or any of the other attendees.

Nancy frowned and looked over her shoulder. Turning back to him, she'd plastered what appeared to be a forced smile on her face. "I heard through the grapevine that you recently bought a horse and buggy." She coyly twirled one of her *kapp* ribbons around her finger like a lovesick schoolgirl. "Now you have everything you need to take a special *maedel* out riding after the singing, *jah*?"

Isaac fought the urge to cringe. Nancy seemed friendly enough, but her forwardness was certainly enough to make any sensible young man think twice about her. Overjoyed that he had a reason to escape her obvious prodding, he said, "*Jah*, I'm seeing Sadie Stolzfus."

Nancy's face suddenly paled. "Oh, I…I didn't know."

A sudden shriek pierced the air, followed by a series of gasps and murmurs. Isaac returned his attention to the volleyball game just in time to see Sadie crumple to the ground after diving for the ball. It seemed like a particularly hard fall, and it was evident that she had injured herself.

Isaac dropped what was left of his snack, rushed past Nancy, sprinted toward the game, then skidded to a halt at Sadie's side. "Are you *oll recht*? Did you hurt yourself?" he asked breathlessly.

"No need to make a fuss. I'm okay," Sadie responded through gritted teeth, clearly trying to minimize her ordeal. "I think I just twisted my ankle." She tried to stand, then promptly lost her balance when she attempted to put weight on her injured foot. Isaac dove to catch her, and he did his best to ignore the rush of heat in his face when she landed perfectly into his protective embrace.

"Careful," Isaac chuckled nervously as he helped Sadie regain her balance. His concern for her remained at the front of his mind, though he found it difficult to ignore the sensation that he'd just been struck by a lightning bolt. Fighting off the strange feeling, he noticed that Sadie was able to stand properly, with most of her weight resting on her uninjured foot.

"I think we've got a crutch you could use, Sadie,"

Pete Graber called from the other side of the volleyball net. "I'll run to the house right quick and fetch it for you." Placing his hand atop his straw hat, Pete dashed for the house.

"Denki," Isaac replied, knowing that a crutch was just what Sadie needed. Noting a bunch of Adirondack chairs under a nearby maple tree, Isaac pointed to the spot. "We'll be sitting under the tree," he called to Pete, but Pete was already out of earshot.

Turning his attention back to Sadie, Isaac let her use his arm to steady herself as they gingerly inched toward the chairs. Truth be told, Isaac absolutely didn't want to see Sadie in any sort of pain, but he was glad to have the chance to spend some quiet time with her in the midst of the youth gathering. *A silver lining*, he told himself inwardly, knowing that time spent with Sadie, whatever the circumstances, would be time well spent.

After being seated under the towering maple tree, checked on by a gaggle of well-meaning friends, and given a crutch by the singing's host, Sadie felt worn out. The pain in her ankle was already starting to lessen, and she didn't relish being fussed over like a sickly child. She glanced at Isaac and noticed him staring down at her injured foot. "Why don't you go join the volleyball game or mingle with some of the others? No need to spoil your time here on account of me being clumsy."

Isaac shook his head so quickly that his straw hat's placement on his head became crooked. "No way, I'd rather stay near you."

"Really?" Sadie's pulse quickened as she wondered if

she had heard Isaac correctly. Surely he only wanted to keep her company so she wouldn't feel alone in a crowd.

"I know what an obstacle an injured ankle can be," Isaac explained as he pointed to her right foot, which she had elevated on one of the empty chairs. "When I was about ten years old, *Mamm* broke her ankle when she fell off a ladder while washing windows. She was in a cast and had to get around on crutches for nearly four months. Wouldn't want you to have to go through that as well."

While Sadie felt blessed and thankful to have a friend who obviously cared about her, she couldn't help but feel disappointed. There simply wasn't a romantic connection that was drawing Isaac to her, and according to his own statement on matters of the heart, that was something that would likely never happen. Doing her best to ignore these feelings, Sadie decided to keep the topic of conversation focused on Isaac's mother.

"It was nice to meet your mother at church," she stated.

His shoulders sagged severely, as if the weight of the world had just come crashing down on him. "Even though she didn't speak to anyone?"

Sadie nodded enthusiastically. "Of course! She is a part of our community now, as are you." She remembered briefly greeting Ruth, Isaac's mother, earlier that day at the church gathering. Though her figure seemed to be too thin, she didn't look ill. Instead, Sadie could see the anguish hidden behind the woman's eyes. It was as if she could almost feel the immense sadness Ruth radiated. Sadie had promptly sent up a prayer that

Isaac's *mamm* would find some joy and peace here in Lancaster County.

Sadie also recalled Isaac mentioning that his mother had become unwell after the death of a loved one, but she hadn't initially realized the extent of Ruth's condition. Although it was never a happy event, losing loved ones was a fact of life. What could have so deeply devastated the dear woman, and how was Isaac able to cope after the same tragedy?

Neither Sadie nor Isaac said anything for a few moments. "Can you think of anything I can do to help your *mamm*?" Sadie finally asked, breaking the somber silence. "Is there anything I can do to help you, Isaac?"

Isaac leaned back against his chair and stared up at the sea of green leaves hanging above them. "That's awful kind of you, but I can't think of anything at the moment." He closed his eyes and sighed before opening them again. "Nothing has changed in two years, so it might just be time for my family and me to accept that this is who *Mamm* is going to be for the rest of her life. To be honest, it's starting to feel hopeless."

"Nothing is hopeless," Sadie replied, eager to encourage her friend.

Isaac crossed his arms over his chest. "You say that because you haven't been through the trauma that we have. How could you possibly say that something like this isn't hopeless?"

Sadie fought the frown that threatened to spread across her face; knowing that Isaac's harsh words were a product of his pain, she didn't take them to heart. She turned her head upward, allowing the sunshine to warm her face. "I know there is hope because *Gott* allowed the sun to rise today. There's still fresh air to breathe, and the birds haven't stopped singing. *Gott* is still providing, even when it's difficult to see it. Where He provides, there is hope."

Isaac's scowl disappeared. "The Lord does indeed provide. He gave me a *wunderbar* friend when I needed one most, and I'm thankful to have you in my life." He reached for Sadie's hand and held it for a few seconds before letting go.

"I'm thankful to have you in my life too, Isaac," Sadie replied as she wished that he hadn't let go of her hand so soon. She was grateful to be able to call him both her friend and her beau, since their unusual relationship had discouraged her parents' matchmaking ultimatum. But still, something deep within her heart reminded Sadie that she would never be fully satisfied until the unlikely day arrived in which she would be swept off her feet by her first and only love.

Chapter Six

After the sun sank into the horizon and the coolness of evening settled in, the fireflies sparkled their way through the darkness. The mugginess of the day melted away as the fresh night air invigorated the Amish youth who still lingered at the Grabers' farm.

When it came time for everyone to head into the barn to begin singing hymns, Sadie had felt deeply moved by the voices joined together in song. By the time the last tune had been sung, her ankle barely hurt at all. It had turned out to be a downright pleasant day, and she was glad to have attended the gathering.

She reached into the bag of marshmallows beside her. She and Rhoda now sat near one of the campfires, roasting them on sticks. Sadie glanced toward Rhoda, who had been silent for quite some time. Rhoda stared into the fire as the marshmallow on the end of her stick turned completely black and was now beginning to smoke. Sadie nudged her friend, causing Rhoda to nearly jump out of her skin.

"Didn't mean to startle you…" Sadie spoke gently. "But you've cooked that marshmallow for so long your stick is about to catch fire."

Snapping out of her daydream, Rhoda instantly pulled the stick from the fire, waving it around and blowing on the marshmallow. Once it was cool enough to touch, she tried to pull it off the stick, but the marshmallow disintegrated into a sticky black mess on her hand. They both laughed until their sides ached.

Once Sadie composed herself, she said what had been on her mind for the past few hours. "You've been kinda quiet tonight," she pointed out while handing her friend a plain handkerchief.

Rhoda accepted the cloth and wiped at the gooey, charred mess on her palm. "*Jah*, I guess I have been."

"Is something bothering you?" Sadie gently pressed, filled with concern for her dear friend.

Rhoda shrugged as she handed the soiled handkerchief back to Sadie. "I'm awful nervous. Tonight will be the first time that Mose and I can spend some time alone." She put her hands to her cheeks, pressing on the hollows. "What if I can't think of anything to say and he thinks I'm boring? What if it's awkward between us?"

Sadie scooted closer to Rhoda and wrapped an arm around her friend. "I reckon you could say nothing the whole ride home, and my twin will still be completely giddy just to spend time with you. I don't think my *bruder* could have chosen a better *aldi*."

Rhoda exhaled quickly through her nose, seeming like she was trying to fight off a smile. "You're exaggerating, but hearing that from someone so close to him does make me feel better. Besides, I'm not his *aldi* yet. This is only our first date." Rhoda pierced a fresh marshmallow onto her stick and dangled it above the flames. "Speaking of courting, I noticed you spending quite a lot of time with that cute Isaac." Rhoda wiggled her auburn eyebrows. "Makes me wonder if you might've found yourself a beau."

Before Sadie could reply, Leah Beiler, another one of Sadie's friends, rushed over to them and took a seat next to Sadie on the log. "Daniel's still not here! He told me he'd be here tonight," she said as she fought to catch her breath, worry etched across her round face.

With the evening almost coming to a close, Leah's beau should have arrived at the Graber farm hours ago. Not wanting to alarm the poor girl, Sadie asked, "Are you sure he isn't around here somewhere? Maybe he's just talking with the menfolk."

Leah shook her head vigorously. "No, he would have come to see me first. I just know that something's wrong!" Her hazel eyes grew shiny with unshed tears. "I'm so worried."

"Of course you are!" Rhoda replied sympathetically, moving to sit on Leah's other side.

"Maybe he took a nap this afternoon and slept right through tonight's activities. You know how Daniel is," Sadie reasoned optimistically. "Remember the time he fell asleep during a church meeting and let out a snore so loud that he woke himself up?"

Leah laughed nervously, her tears spilling down her cheeks. "You're right." She dabbed at the wetness on her face. "He's never done anything like this before, so I'm very concerned."

"Leah, really," Nancy Beiler groaned as she lowered herself onto the adjacent log seat. "Pull yourself together. You shouldn't immediately assume the worst."

Sadie's mouth dropped open at Nancy's curtness toward her own sister. Was she attempting to show tough love, or was she brushing off Leah's legitimate alarm? Sadie focused her attention back on Leah. "Nancy is right. Try not to worry too much. If he doesn't show up within the next few minutes, I'm sure we can ask some of the men to go to Daniel's house and find out where he is." She gingerly placed her hand against Leah's clammy cheek. "If there is anything I can do to help, please let me know."

"*Denki*, Sadie," Leah quickly replied, "but please don't ruin your evening on my account. If you had plans to go for a buggy ride tonight with someone special, do that. If my beau doesn't show up, I'll ask my brother to stop by Daniel's place as he takes his date home."

"That's right," Nancy chimed in with a squeak as she leaned closer to the group. "Daniel will be fine. Besides, I heard that single Sadie isn't single anymore, so she will indeed be out riding tonight with her new beau."

Sadie turned her face away from her peers. Nancy's words were sarcastic and cruel. She knew that she was rapidly becoming the topic of whispers and the subject of pity in their district. Quite honestly, she yearned to remind Nancy that though several of the young men had taken her out, none of them had stuck around for more than one date once they'd realized her true colors. Instead, she sniffled quietly, listening to the fire crackle and snap.

"I suppose it's nice that Isaac fancies you over the other single women, but he's new to the area and hasn't realized how…unique you are," Nancy went on, her insincere smile front and center on her face.

"Of course Sadie caught Isaac's eye," Rhoda replied, sticking up for Sadie as her eyes narrowed into thin slits. "She's sweet as shoofly pie and she's the best friend anyone could ever hope for."

"It sounds like maybe you're a little jealous, *schwester*," added Leah quietly, as if afraid to disagree with her elder sibling.

"I'm not at all jealous," Nancy chuckled as her hand flew to her chest in self-defense. "Isaac just seems like such a mature fellow with a good head on his shoulders, and Sadie is very free-spirited. What normal Amish fellow would be interested in a grown woman who would sooner be found up a tree or picking wildflowers instead of baking a pie or sewing a quilt for her loved ones?"

"I would."

The four women turned to see Isaac emerging from the darkness with a stern frown across his face. He marched right up to Nancy and glared at her. "I would rather court a woman with a wildfire spirit and a heart the size of Lancaster County than one who's pushy and judgmental. Maybe you should take a lesson from Sadie and learn to treat others with kindness." Nancy's mouth dropped open before she sheepishly rose from her seat and scurried away from the group.

Isaac turned toward the other three women, allowing

his expression to soften. "Do you know where I could find Leah Beiler? Some guy named Daniel just showed up, and he's looking for her."

"That's me." Leah stood as relief flooded her face. "Where is he?" Isaac told Leah and she promptly took off to find him.

Finally, Isaac turned to Sadie. "It's getting kind of late," he said with a crooked grin as he extended his hand to her. "Could I give you a ride home?"

Feeling as if she had been rescued from the jaws of a lion, Sadie smiled sweetly up at Isaac. She accepted his hand, stood from her seat next to Rhoda and bid her friend farewell. As they walked slowly toward the Graber barnyard, where Isaac's horse and buggy were already hitched and ready to go, Sadie marveled at how Isaac's sudden appearance at the campfire had instantly removed the negativity and embarrassment that Nancy had shoveled onto her. He'd let it be known that she was worthy of love, just the way that the Lord had created her to be. A feeling of safety enveloped her like a warm blanket, and at that moment, Sadie knew that she and Isaac would be lifelong friends.

With only the moonlight and a battery-powered buggy headlight guiding their way, Isaac trusted that Shadow would know the road to Sadie's home better than he did. This was his first nighttime outing since moving to Lancaster County, and he was disoriented on the silent country roads, surrounded by the shadows of whispering cornstalks. It was his job to ensure that Sadie was returned home safely, and he needed to see it through.

As Shadow pulled the rig down North Weavertown Road at a steady pace, Isaac attempted to shake off the unsettling feeling that he'd allowed to consume him.

After pitifully grieving for what felt like the longest time, Isaac finally came to accept his fiancée's death, deciding that she wouldn't want him to carry on mournfully for the rest of his days. Still, Daniel's talk of the roadside disaster he'd witnessed before arriving at the gathering was enough to stir up the dust of sorrow that never seemed to fully settle.

"*Denki* for standing up for me tonight" came Sadie's voice from the passenger's side of the buggy. As gentle as it was, her words still managed to startle Isaac. They hadn't spoken much since leaving the youth gathering, and in that time Isaac had gotten lost in thought.

"You're welcome," he replied, though he wasn't in the mood to have a conversation.

"It made me feel a lot better after Nancy was unkind to me," Sadie went on.

"*Jah*, I guess so."

A few seconds of silence passed before Sadie spoke up again. "Is everything all right, Isaac? You seemed to be enjoying yourself most of the day, at least until you came to save me from Nancy." There was a hint of anxious sadness in Sadie's tone. "Are you maybe wishing you didn't have to take me home tonight?"

Sadie's question tugged on Isaac's heartstrings. "*Nee*, of course not," he replied, sincerely hoping that she was reassured of how much he enjoyed her company. "I'm honored to be your beau and see that you get home safely."

Sadie seemed to mull that over for a spell. "Then why are you being so quiet?"

Isaac heaved a heavy sigh, then began to explain. "While you were talking with your friends, some of the other guys and I were shooting the breeze. When that Daniel fellow showed up, he told us that he'd witnessed a car clip the side of a passing buggy, which flipped the rig, so he stayed to help the family inside."

Sadie gasped. "I hope no one was injured!"

"Thankfully, Daniel reported that everyone in the buggy was unharmed."

"And you're feeling down because of this story Daniel told?"

Isaac chewed on his tongue, dreading reliving the memories that he was about to share. "I think it's time I tell you the full story of what caused *Mamm* and me to come to Bird-in-Hand for an extended visit." Even though the night air was pleasantly cool, Isaac shivered as if a bitter winter wind had just whipped through the buggy.

"I was once betrothed. Her name was Rebecca King, and I loved her ever since we were *kinner*. She was smart, beautiful and very kind." A lump formed in Isaac's throat that he could not swallow. "Sorry," he apologized as he choked back a sob. He cleared his throat several times to keep his tears at bay. As Isaac gripped Shadow's reins, he felt Sadie's cool, soft hand remove one of his from his white-knuckled grasp on the leather ropes. Tenderly, she took his strong, callused hand and held it in hers. In the light of the moon, Isaac could see that she was gazing at him with a calm but concerned smile.

Sadie's comforting touch effortlessly pierced through even his strongest barrier, and Isaac could no longer restrain his tears. "Rebecca wasn't just my *aldi*, she was my whole world. She was a part of our family even though we never got the chance to get married." His voice cracked, and he tried to regain his composure. "She was close to *Mamm*, too, and they visited with each other every Friday. They would bake all kinds of different pies, cakes…you name it. Seemed like they found a new recipe every week, and the rest of our household sure did enjoy that." Isaac grinned somberly at the memory.

Sadie continued to hold his hand as Isaac went on. "One afternoon, Rebecca was already on her way to visit *Mamm* when a severe storm rolled up. I wish… I wish she'd done the sensible thing and turned back to go home when the weather got bad." Briefly letting go of the reins, Isaac wiped his eyes. He took a shaky breath and exhaled through pursed lips. Taking hold of Shadow's reins with his free hand, he sighed and went on.

"*Mamm* saw that it had started to rain, so she ran out to our front porch, where we have our clothesline attached. She was taking the dry laundry off the line before it could get soaked when she saw Rebecca coming up the lane on her scooter, right in the middle of the worst of the storm."

Isaac paused, wondering why he was suddenly spilling his soul to Sadie, who had still not let go of his hand.

He'd lost his place in the story and mentally backtracked to where he'd left off. "A car was coming up the road. The driver was distracted by their phone, or so I was told. They were speeding and ran into Rebecca." Isaac heard Sadie sharply inhale, but she didn't interrupt him. "The impact threw her into our yard. Seeing what happened, *Mamm* ran to help Rebecca."

Isaac was silent for several more minutes, as was Sadie. Without realizing he was doing so, he gripped her hand tighter, needing her support.

"*Daed* and I were in the woodworking shop when we heard *Mamm*'s screams. We found *Mamm* kneeling beside Rebecca, wailing uncontrollably. I took off on foot toward the phone shanty at the end of our lane, and I called for help. An ambulance had already arrived by the time I ran back. The paramedics told us that Rebecca had died on impact." He gulped, swallowing against the bitter bile rising in his throat. "*Mamm* was barely able to tell my *daed* what had happened, but when she did, he later relayed the information to me. After she recounted what she'd seen, *Mamm* stopped speaking, and hasn't said a single word since that day."

"I'm so sorry to hear about all the pain that you and your *mamm* have suffered," Sadie whispered, gently touching the side of Isaac's face and wiping away his tears. "From what you've told me, it sounds like Rebecca was a woman after the Lord's own heart. No wonder you and your *mamm* cared for her so much!"

"*Jah*, she was. So when Daniel told us about the accident he'd witnessed tonight, it reminded me of that awful time in my life, in my family's lives. Rainy days are painful, too, since it stirs up memories of a day that we'd all rather forget."

Sadie squeezed Isaac's hand. "I understand. I can't imagine your loss." As if carrying the weight of their conversation, she took a great breath. "After *Gott* sent the rain to Noah, he put his rainbow in the sky. Don't get caught up in the storm clouds, because there's still hope for something beautiful on the other side of the storm."

Stunned by Sadie's gracious wisdom, Isaac suddenly felt lighter. "I know you're right. The initial sting of grief has lessened over time, and I know Rebecca would be pleased that I'm making a life for myself, and taking care of *Mamm* too."

Sadie seemed to ponder this last point. "So you and your *mamm* moved to Bird-in-Hand to encourage her healing with new surroundings?"

"That's right," Isaac confirmed, turning Shadow down the Stolzfuses' long driveway. He slowed the gelding's pace to a walk, trying to prolong this moment with Sadie. He wasn't ready to say good-night, not when he'd just bared the entirety of his soul to her. There was something mighty calming about her honest presence, and though he was slightly embarrassed, Isaac didn't regret falling to pieces in front of this lovely, unique woman.

They made pleasant small talk until they neared the white Stolzfus barn, where Sadie requested to be dropped off so the noise of the buggy wouldn't wake the sleeping household.

"Sadie," Isaac called quietly to stop her as she exited the buggy. "I…uh…I'm real glad to have spent time with you today." He felt his heart start to beat a little faster as the moonlight illuminated Sadie's lovely eyes.

A smile bloomed on Sadie's face. "*Jah*, me too. I'll look forward to seeing you again real soon." She thanked Isaac for the ride and scurried toward her father's two-story stone farmhouse.

"Good night," Isaac replied, wondering if the twinkle in Sadie's eyes had been a reflection of the moonlight or perhaps a touch more. He felt something almost magnetic growing between him and Sadie. Maybe she'd felt the same emotional bond. After tonight's conversation, Isaac had to admit that he felt closer to Sadie than anyone else in his life, and he wondered how he'd managed to survive these past two years without her.

Chapter Seven

After the noon meal was eaten and the dishes were washed, Sadie padded down the dirt buggy lane that connected neighboring farms with a plate of freshly baked chocolate chip cookies in hand. On this cloudless day, Sadie was headed to Miriam Fisher's house. She'd baked the cookies for Isaac as a symbol of their friendship, though her true motive was to ensure that Isaac was in better spirits. Sadie was the least talented baker in her family, so the cookies were lumpy. The one she'd sampled had tasted just fine, so she hoped Isaac and his family would enjoy them anyway.

Continuing down the lane, Sadie recalled last night's surprising turn of events. She'd never imagined that she would have a beau to drive her home from the youth gathering. It was equally surprising that Isaac had shed some tears in front of her. The story of his fiancée's death, and how it affected his poor mother, pained Sadie. No wonder he wasn't interested in finding a wife again, Sadie thought as the buggy lane led her to the edge of Orchard Road.

When she arrived at the Fisher house, Sadie noticed Mim seated on a bench under a weeping willow tree with a small group of children at her feet, both Amish and *Englisch* alike. Children from the area often flocked to Mim as if she were the neighborhood grandmother, and she clearly enjoyed their company as much as the children enjoyed hers. The dear woman was animatedly recounting the Bible story of Jonah and the whale, and the eager listeners watched intently, with some of their little mouths hanging open.

Sadie waved to get her attention. "Sorry to interrupt your story," she greeted Mim and the group of children as she approached. "Sounds like a whale of a tale." Mim chuckled at Sadie's pun.

"*Jah*, Mim's telling us about how the Lord sent a great big fish to swallow up Jonah when he was running away!" Leroy Mast, a child from one of the neighboring farms, keenly reported to Sadie, his miniature straw hat tumbling off his copper-colored hair when he mentioned the whale's size.

Sadie giggled. "That's one of my favorite stories." Smiling at all of the children, she gently tapped the tip of Leroy's freckled nose. "We always get in trouble when we run from *Gott*'s will."

"*Ach*, Sadie." Leroy gleefully squirmed. "That may be so, but I ain't never heard of anyone getting swallowed by a fish 'cause of it!"

This caused a loud burst of laughter to ripple through the group of children. Mim and Sadie also chortled at the honest remark from young Leroy. When things settled down, Sadie explained that she was searching for Isaac.

"He just left for the farm supply store," Mim regretfully informed Sadie. "You can leave it on the kitchen table and I'll let him know you stopped by when he returns."

"*Denki*, Mim. I'll do just that." Sadie bid goodbye to the caring woman and the children gathered at her feet. She bounded up the porch stairs, walked through the front door and entered Mim's tidy kitchen, where the scents of cinnamon and apples filled the air. She sniffed at the enticing aroma as she placed the plate of cookies on the kitchen table. As she turned and headed for the door, in the adjacent sitting room she saw a frail-looking woman seated in a rocking chair that faced a window.

Sadie was startled by someone else's presence in the otherwise empty house. After meeting the woman during a church meeting, Sadie instantly recognized Isaac's mother, Ruth. She longed to visit with her, wishing so desperately to heal her hurting heart, but she reminded herself that only the Lord could truly provide healing. Was it wise to disturb the bereaved woman, even if only to say hello?

Ignoring the initial hesitation she felt, Sadie walked into the room and gently knocked on the light green wall so she wouldn't frighten her. Ruth looked up from her chair, a bit of surprise crossing her face.

"Hello, Ruth." Sadie spoke softly as she approached the deeply grieved woman. "It's me, Sadie Stolzfus. It's nice to see you again." Sadie carefully tempered the cheer in her tone, wanting to avoid overwhelming Isaac's fragile mother.

Ruth's bluish-gray eyes glanced toward Sadie, but she didn't make eye contact. She didn't reply, and Sadie didn't expect her to. The woman's golden hair, similar to Sadie's own, seemed dulled, causing Sadie to wonder if the woman's lackluster locks and thin frame were a side effect of the trauma she'd experienced.

Sadie took a seat on the sofa next to Ruth's rocking chair. When she was settled, Ruth returned her gaze to her folded hands. "We're awful glad to have you and Isaac here in Bird-in-Hand with us," Sadie ventured truthfully. She was tempted to ask how Ruth liked living in this part of the country, but quickly nixed the idea. It was probably better not to ask any questions, she decided, worried that Ruth might feel pressured to respond.

Realizing that she hadn't offered Ruth a cookie, Sadie excused herself to retrieve the plate she'd left in the kitchen. When she returned, she presented the strange-looking cookies to Ruth. "I made these for Isaac." Sadie held the plate closer for Ruth's inspection. "They look a little funny, but they taste all right. Would you like to try one?"

Ruth shook her head ever so slightly. "That's okay," Sadie reassured her. "I'll leave them right here in case you change your mind, but I think I'm going to have one now." Sadie popped a cookie into her mouth as she once again seated herself next to Ruth. As she chewed, Sadie noticed a book about gardening lying against Ruth's chair. "May I have a look at this?" Of course, Ruth didn't respond, but Sadie didn't feel right about picking it up without asking for her permission.

She waited for a few seconds and when Ruth's disposition didn't change, Sadie reached for the hardcover book and thumbed through the glossy pages. "I enjoy gardening too. I've worked at our local greenhouse since I was fifteen." She continued to flip through the book and noticed that the first page of the chapter about perennials was dog-eared. "I love perennials too. They're downright faithful, ain't so? Blooming year after year just as sure as the sun rises each morning."

Sadie noticed when Ruth leaned closer ever so slightly. Her visibly tired eyes settled on the page Sadie had turned to. Seeing this, Sadie scooted over to one side of the couch and patted the cushion next to her. "Come sit by me!"

To Sadie's pleasant surprise, Ruth slowly rose from her chair and took a spot next to her on the sofa. When she was seated, Sadie handed Ruth the left side of the book as she held the right. She chattered on and on, pointing out different plants, describing some as stubborn and others as easy-breezy.

Sadie noticed that Ruth's gaze lingered on a picture of purple asters. She ran her fingers over the picture, and for the slightest moment, her dull eyes looked more blue than gray.

"You like those flowers? Those are one of my favorites too," Sadie exclaimed, taking hold of Ruth's hand, giving it a few light squeezes. "I knew that you and I would be friends."

For the first time since Sadie had introduced herself,

Ruth's eyes met hers. They were drained, but Sadie thought maybe they were smiling at her. All anyone really needed was an understanding heart to hold their hand, and Sadie was honored to be that person for Ruth.

The screen door squeaked open as Mim entered her kitchen. She did a double take when she saw Sadie and Ruth sitting on the sofa together as if they were life-long friends. "Sadie, I didn't know you were still here. I sent the *kinner* home since it looks like it could start making down any minute now."

Sadie's brow furrowed at Mim's mention of rain. She leaned around Ruth to glimpse out the window and saw dark clouds gathering on the horizon. "I guess that's the Lord nudging me to hurry on home."

Mim insisted that she wait until the rain passed, but Sadie declined, informing Mim that it was her duty to prepare an afternoon snack for her younger sister, Susannah, while the girl finished her chores. "There'll be a mighty price to pay if I don't have something on the table for her." Mim's laughter reverberated through the house at Sadie's implication, though the sound caused Ruth to wince.

Sadie stood, feeling a strain on her arm. Ruth was still clutching her hand, like a child who was afraid to be separated from her mother in a crowd. Filled with compassion for the dear woman, Sadie squatted to her eye level. "Thank you for spending some time with me. I'll come back to visit real soon."

Ruth nodded with just the slightest head movement, accepting Sadie's kind words. Sadie squeezed Ruth's hand a few times, then headed for the door, Mim scurrying behind her.

When the two women stepped outside onto the covered porch, Mim closed both the heavy wooden door and the screen door behind her. "*Denki* for taking time out of your day for my *schwester*," Mim sighed. "Poor thing is so gloomy that I fear she scares some folks away."

A puzzled expression swept across Sadie's face. "Why would anyone be afraid of someone who's suffering?"

Mim beamed warmly at Sadie as she gently cradled her palm against her young friend's cheek. "Because, dear one, not all farmers know how to tend black sheep."

Sadie bobbed her head, understanding the proverb. She looked down at the ground as an idea formed in her mind. "We were looking through her gardening book, and she seemed to enjoy it. Do you think she'd like to plant some flowers with me?"

Mim shook her graying head. "Awful nice of you, but I can't imagine that she'd willingly go anywhere for the sake of socializing. It takes a whole lot of tender coaxing just to get her to attend the biweekly church services."

Sadie mulled that over, twisting one of her *kapp* ribbons around her finger. "She doesn't have to come to my house. What if I brought some flowers from the greenhouse over here? You think she'd be willing to come outside and help me plant them?"

Mim shrugged. "We do have a flower bed that's been empty so far this year. I suspect you know not to get your hopes up when it comes to Ruth, but it can't hurt to give it a try."

* * *

That evening, after running some errands, caring for all of Mim's animals and giving Shadow a thorough bath, Isaac entered the fragrant kitchen. Hearing the screen door shut behind him, Mim grinned and pushed her foggy glasses from the tip of her nose to the bridge. "You must have known that supper's almost ready, *jah*?"

"If my brain didn't tell me, my stomach sure would have." Isaac patted his middle like he always had since his boyhood days.

"There's a plate of chocolate chip cookies over on the counter." Mim jerked her head in the direction of the sweet snacks. "Better have a few of those, so you don't bite my hands off when I put the food on the table."

Isaac sarcastically scoffed at his aunt, who threw her head back in laughter. Then he moseyed over to the plate of cookies and was taken aback to see that they looked less than tasty. Some of them were tiny and nearly burnt black. Others were orb-like, and couldn't have possibly been baked thoroughly. One seemed particularly lumpy, and another seemed like it had no chocolate chips at all.

Bewildered, Isaac stared at the plate. "Mim, did you bake these today?"

"No, Sadie Stolzfus came over a few hours ago and brought them for you as a gift." Mim plated a few freshly baked dinner rolls and brought them to the table. "Looks like you may have found yourself a sweetheart here in Bird-in-Hand after all."

"*Jah*, I have been seeing Sadie," Isaac admitted,

though he chose not to mention that their courtship was merely one of convenience.

"I thought that might be the case," Mim responded in a singsong voice. "Anyway, your *mamm* and I ate some of them, and we're both still alive."

"Well, I suppose I'll try just one." Isaac selected the largest cookie, sniffed it hesitantly, then took a bite. Instantly he was surprised by the delicious flavor. Once he gobbled down the first cookie, he reached for two more.

"Don't eat so much that you spoil your supper," Mim chided him, flicking her dishcloth against his arm. "Go get your *mamm* and let her know supper's ready, would you?"

Isaac nodded as he finished eating the cookies. "Sure will, but who knows if she'll actually eat anything. She picks at meals like a bird."

"Well, after Sadie spent some time with her this afternoon, your *mamm* perked up so much that she ate a few of Sadie's cookies. I don't think I've seen her snack since you two moved into this house."

Isaac spun around, feeling his heart rate increase. "Sadie spent time with *Mamm*?"

"*Jah*, I was outside reading to some *kinner* when she stopped by to drop off her cookies. I went inside, oh, about a half hour later. She and your *mamm* were like two peas in a pod, sitting together and looking through that gardening book."

Isaac smiled broadly, his heart warmed at the image that Mim planted in his mind's eye. "*Mamm* didn't seem overwhelmed? Sadie can be...you know...a lot."

Mim stifled a laugh, putting her fingers to her lips.

"From what I saw, Sadie's quirks might be the perfect remedy for your *mamm*'s condition."

Both comforted and intrigued by Mim's response, Isaac gazed back down at the plate of Sadie's unusual cookies. Not only had the strange girl comforted him during his painful memories, but she also had some sort of positive effect on his sorrowful mother. With an overwhelming need to see Sadie again, Isaac decided to take a ride over to the Stolzfus place after supper.

"There's a visitor downstairs who's asking to see you."

Sadie opened her eyes when she heard a knock on her bedroom door and her sister's high voice. She'd decided to take a short rest on her bed before it was time for the evening milking, but she hadn't planned on falling asleep. She rubbed her eyes and rose to meet Susannah at the door. "Someone's here for me? Who is it?"

"It's that fellow that we met at church on Sunday," Susannah gushed with rosy cheeks. "The same one who brought you home from the singing. If I didn't know better, I'd say that he's your beau."

Sadie felt a flutter of excitement in her chest that outweighed her annoyance that Susannah had stayed up late last night to spy on her. Knowing she would need to have a talk with her thirteen-year-old sister later, Sadie burst out of her bedroom with Susannah on her heels. "Did Isaac say what he wanted?" Sadie asked, taking the stairs two at a time. She hadn't expected a visit from him today, and as thrilling as his sudden arrival was, she also worried that something might be wrong.

"*Nee*, just asked if you were home."

When the sisters reached the bottom of the stairs, Sadie thought she would faint at the sight of Isaac standing there, right in the middle of the kitchen. When he turned toward her, he smiled warmly. Since he was unmarried, he was always clean-shaven, but a small amount of stubble on the lower half of his face gave him an attractive, masculine appearance. "Hiya, Sadie. Could we chat privately for a spell?"

Sadie glanced at her curious sister and couldn't help but grin. "*Jah*, of course. Follow me." She led Isaac out of the house and to an iron bench between a pair of weeping willows that looked over the small stream that wove through the farm. Though there would be an hour or two of daylight left, the moon was already high in the purplish sky. When they were seated side by side, far away from eavesdropping ears, Sadie finally felt free to speak. "Wasn't expecting to see you today, but I'm glad you're here. Is everything all right?"

Isaac took off his straw hat, hung it on one of his knees, then turned to smile at Sadie. "*Jah*, I wanted to thank you for your cookies."

Sadie smiled back. "You came all the way over here just to say *denki*?"

Isaac's head bobbed. "*Jah*, they were mighty tasty."

Sadie's eyes widened in surprise. "Really? They tasted all right to me, but I was afraid you wouldn't eat them since they were so odd-looking."

"*Mamm*, Mim and I polished them all off. I wish there were more!" After Sadie stopped chuckling at Isaac's enthusiasm, he went on. "I wish you had more faith in your abilities, Sadie. The cookies were delicious, even if they did look a bit strange. I'm sure with some practice they could look as good as they taste."

Sadie shrugged. Others had encouraged her to hone her cooking and baking skills, but since these were of no interest to her, she saw no need. "I don't think so. Besides, folks know I'm somewhat useless in the kitchen, so only the bravest souls would be willing to try anything I make."

Isaac studied her intently, as if he cared very deeply about their conversation. "Different doesn't mean useless. I enjoyed your baking, and I think you should keep practicing."

Sadie knew Isaac's gentle coaxing was only for her benefit. She was a grown woman, and it was about time for her to start putting more care into household duties. Besides, how could she turn Isaac down, especially with the cute way he smiled at her? "I'll think about it," Sadie finally agreed with a wink.

Isaac's smile widened. He leaned forward, then said, "Speaking of *Mamm*, I heard you spent some time with her today."

Sadie nervously chewed on her bottom lip. "*Jah*, I spent some time with her talking about gardening. Did I overstep a boundary?"

"*Nee*, not at all," Isaac replied, much to Sadie's relief. "In fact, *Mamm* perked up and ate more than usual at suppertime. Seems like your visit had a very positive effect on her." He paused, clasping his hands together and staring at the neatly manicured grass beneath their feet. "I was just wondering how you managed to break through to her. I mean, you're practically a stranger to her, yet you were able to get her to eat a decent meal when no one else could."

Sadie grinned, pleased to hear that Isaac's mother was feeling a bit better. "I don't know. I just talked to her." She gazed into the gentle water that babbled over the stones in the stream, thinking of how to best describe what was in her heart. "Maybe she just needed someone who wouldn't expect anything from her. Maybe she needs to just be who she is right now, with no pressure to change."

Isaac nodded, taking in everything Sadie had to say. "Well, you could be right. As her family, we're very anxious to see her get back to her old self. I'll have to try to give her the time and space she needs." He let out a small sigh, then inhaled some of the cool evening air scented by a recently cut and raked hayfield. "Well," he said as he placed his hat back on his head, "I better get going. I just wanted to stop by to say thanks for the cookies and for spending time with my *mudder*."

After Isaac climbed back into his buggy and headed for home, Sadie lingered outdoors for a while. She took several deep breaths, reminding herself that Isaac valued their unique friendship. And that it was only a friendship, despite his sweet smiles and looks. Despite her growing interest in the handsome newcomer, she forced herself to remember that their courtship was only pretend.

Chapter Eight

Sadie pulled her small wagon behind her as she journeyed to visit with Isaac's mother, glad that she could make use of the favorite childhood toy. The little green wagon, crafted by her father nearly two decades ago, was full of bright red geraniums, gold marigolds and bubblegum-pink petunias. Since it was the middle of August, the stock of summer flowers at the greenhouse was significantly dwindling and being replaced with infant autumnal plants. Since these colorful summer flowers were part of an end-of-the-season sale, she'd purchased them for barely a few dollars after her employee discount was added in.

With the wagon wheels squeaking behind her, Sadie hummed a hymn to herself as she walked down Mim's driveway, then around to the back of the old farmhouse. Ruth was sitting on the covered porch, sheltered from the sweltering noon sun. While most of the Amish women in the area wore dresses made from solid-colored fabric ranging in shades of green, blue and purple, Ruth's dress was a mousy color and seemed two sizes too large for her.

"Hello," Sadie called with a friendly wave, stopping at the base of the porch stairs. "Look what I've brought for you!" She turned and gestured to the wagonload of flowers. "I was hoping that you might want to plant them with me."

Ruth leaned forward slightly, peering through the whitewashed spokes that supported the porch railing. When her gaze reached the plants, her eyes brightened, but she didn't get up.

In respect for Ruth's state, Sadie slowly ascended the steps, then peeked into the open window. "Mim, it's Sadie!"

A few seconds later, Mim came to the window and peered outside, smiling to beat the band. "Hiya, Sadie. Isaac's out in the barn, if you came looking for him." She held a mixing bowl in one hand and a wooden spoon in the other, never stopping her stirring.

Sadie felt her cheeks flush. "I'm here to see Ruth," she replied, though the possibility of running into Isaac was certainly a bonus. "I brought some flowers. Is it all right if we make use of your flower bed today?"

Mim's smile faded slightly upon hearing Sadie's request and she stopped stirring whatever she was whipping up in her mixing bowl. She and Sadie gazed knowingly at each other, both understanding that Ruth would probably refuse to participate. Eventually, Mim bobbed her head and resumed her stirring. "That sounds right nice. I haven't gotten to it this year, and the old patch of dirt could use some prettying up."

Sadie thanked Mim, then bounded over to Ruth, the wooden porch creaking beneath her steps. "C'mon, Ruth, let's go get these flowers planted in their new home." She extended her hand to the seated, troubled woman, patiently wondering if she would accept. Ruth weakly took Sadie's hand and rose from her seat with the slowness of a woman twice her age. Hand in hand, the two women padded down the porch steps and onto the neatly mowed grass. Sadie used her free hand to grasp the wagon handle and led Ruth to the large circular plot of dirt in the house's side yard. Ruth certainly wasn't a large woman, but Sadie still felt heaviness as Ruth linked arms with her. Sadie wondered if perhaps she was feeling the weight of Ruth's depressed spirit, and she hoped that the sight of the new flowers would cheer the woman up.

"Would you like me to bring your chair over here?" Sadie offered, wanting to be absolutely sure that Ruth felt at ease. Ruth didn't reply, of course, but she cautiously lowered herself into the grass at the edge of the flower bed. Much less gracefully, Sadie dropped to her knees and grinned at Ruth. "I'd rather sit in the grass too! There's something good for the soul about being so close to *Gott*'s earth, don't you think?"

Crawling next to her wagon, Sadie retrieved a few of the flowers and her gardening tools. She crawled back to Ruth and placed the tools and flowers between them so Ruth could choose to join in without pressure. Sadie reached for her handheld cultivator and began digging into the hardened dirt, which hadn't been broken since the previous year's spring. She continued loosening the soil, disrupting the cement-like top layer of dirt in front of them. "Seems like the Lord's earth matches His people, ain't so? Sometimes there's a hard exterior that protects all the good stuff hidden away under it." She glanced over her shoulder, watching Ruth's unchanging brooding expression.

Once the dormant flower bed had been fully tilled by hand, Sadie dug her hands into the rich, moist soil, plucking away a few rocks and weeds. "I guess I'm guilty of it myself." She leaned back on her heels, wiping her forehead with her forearm. "People expect certain things of girls my age, things that I don't know if I'll ever live up to." Sadie looked up, closing her eyes and letting the sun's warmth caress her cheeks. When she opened her eyes, she looked toward Ruth, who gazed back at her sympathetically.

Sadie covered Ruth's clammy hand with her dirt-covered one, hoping Isaac's mother wouldn't mind her muddy touch. "Sometimes we get so done in by expectations, or worries, or grief, that our ground hardens right up and not a single flower can grow." At this, Ruth looked away, her hand stirring under Sadie's. "If we allow our Heavenly Father, the ultimate gardener, to till up our hardened hearts, He can plant a whole new garden, one that doesn't turn brown and wither away during difficult seasons. Then life can once again become as vibrant as these flowers."

Ruth sniffled, using her black apron to dab at the corners of her eyes. She looked back to Sadie, her eyes shiny and the corners of her mouth turned slightly upward. She reached out, touching the side of Sadie's face, so gently that Sadie barely felt Ruth's fingertips brush against her cheek. Sadie smiled in return, hoping with all her might that her words were of some encouragement to the woman whose heart wept more than anyone's ever should.

A few moments later, Ruth pushed the sleeves of her dress up to her elbows and plunged her hands into the dirt, letting them sink in. Wrist-deep in the soil, Ruth worked her fingers into the earth, staring into the brown, soft ground with childlike wonder. Perhaps that soil was the first thing she'd allowed herself to feel, other than sorrow, in a very long time, Sadie thought to herself.

Isaac stood next to the barn's side door with a small can of white paint in one hand and a brush in the other. He took a few steps back to survey the work he had done. The fresh paint job seemed a bit uneven. He reached high to add another coat to an area where the paint seemed too thin. Honestly, he was disappointed that his work wasn't living up to his usual high standards.

What was going on with him today? He glanced over his shoulder to steal another peek at Sadie as she and his mother knelt near a previously barren flower bed, planting a variety of colorful flowers together. He could see that color was returning to his mother's pale face, and a gorgeous smile was blooming on Sadie's face. As he took in the scene, Sadie looked up from the flowers, beaming at him. Caught staring, Isaac sheepishly smiled back, then quickly returned to his painting.

When the second coat of paint had been completed, Isaac decided that he could use a break. He chuckled to himself, knowing that he could normally work much longer before needing a rest, but Sadie's nearby presence beckoned for him to visit with her. He made quick work of rinsing his paintbrush and hammering the paint can's lid back into place, then hurried toward the flower bed.

"Wow, you two really spruced up this old heap of dirt," Isaac declared, planting his hands on his hips. He whistled as he took in the sight of the freshly planted geraniums, marigolds and petunias. "Never seen Mim's yard look so pretty."

Sadie grinned, then looked away, as if his indirect compliment had caught her off guard. She turned to Ruth and patted her hand. "Well, the Lord created these lovely flowers. All your *mamm* and I did was plant them, and we had a real *gut* time doing so!"

Ruth gazed at Sadie lovingly. Though her lips didn't form a full smile, Isaac noticed that the corners of her mouth were turned slightly upward, and her eyes had more life in them than they'd had since Rebecca's passing.

"I agree with my nephew," Mim called as she approached with a jug in one hand and several paper cups in the other. "When it was just me living here alone, I couldn't find time to plant beautiful flowers." She took a moment to catch her breath when she reached the flower bed. "I appreciate you two bringing some color to my yard, as well as all the repairs you are making in the barn, Isaac, though you best clean yourself up before stepping foot back into my house!"

From her seat on the ground, Sadie looked up at Isaac and started to laugh. "Looks like you've gained some freckles since I've seen you last!"

Isaac curiously reached up to touch his face and felt some small, tacky paint drops on his forehead. "I guess I got a bit overzealous with my painting."

"You sure did," Mim replied, "which is why I brought some meadow tea out. I'm sure you could all use a cool drink." She handed a cup to her sister, Sadie and Isaac, then filled each with the refreshing beverage. "Why don't you all come sit on the porch and get out of the sun for a spell?"

Everyone agreed. Isaac was pleased to see that Sadie helped his mother up from her place on the ground and walked at her slow place until they were seated in the shade of the porch. It was clear that she cared a great deal about those around her, and Isaac found that to be a very attractive quality.

"Mim, speaking of the barn, I wonder if you'd ever considered building a larger one," Isaac asked as he gently glided back and forth in one of the white wicker rocking chairs.

Mim's forehead creased as she sipped on what little meadow tea was left in her cup. "What for?"

"The repairs I've been making out there got me thinking that the building is awful small. It's really only a stable. There's just enough room for your two cows, your horse and mine. You have a good-sized parcel of land here. If you decided to farm it, you'd need a lot more barn space."

"*Ach*, definitely not. I'm getting up in years and have

no intention of starting to farm now," Mim replied with a wave of her hand.

"I could farm it for you," Isaac offered hopefully. "If we added on to your barn, I could get started next spring." He glanced over at Sadie, who looked back at him with a twinkle in her eye. They'd discussed his dream of making a living as a farmer several times, but with his job at his father's woodworking shop, the chance of that was slim to none.

"I don't think so, Isaac. Who knows how long you and my *schwester* will be staying here with me. It would be a shame to build a big barn only to have you two move back home, and then I would have no use for it."

Isaac wanted nothing more than for his mother to recover from her severe depression, but the thought of heading home to Indiana didn't sit well with him. He glanced over again at Sadie, noticing that Mim's words had also caused her to frown. Was she disappointed that Isaac wouldn't be getting the opportunity to farm as he wanted, or was she also upset by the idea of him eventually returning home? Bird-in-Hand was starting to feel like where he belonged, and Isaac knew that this feeling was a result of the unique bond he had with Sadie.

"Mim—" Sadie suddenly spoke up "—what if you were to just build on to the existing barn? Then you'd have a place for visitors' horses to rest without having to wait outside, still hitched to their buggies. You could also store your buggy in there to keep it out of the elements. We could have a partial barn raising, which would be much less expensive than starting from scratch!"

"Jah," Isaac agreed, excited by Sadie's suggestion.

"I'd even be willing to split the cost of the lumber with you. Plus, it would be a nice get-together for the community before harvesttime."

Mim smiled coyly, her eyes darting between Sadie and Isaac. "If I didn't know better, I'd think that you two planned this attack on me." Both Sadie and Isaac opened their mouths to deny her insinuation, but Mim held up her hand to stop them. "Spread the word! In a week or two, we'll have ourselves a partial barn raising."

Sadie and Isaac both let out a celebratory whoop. Mim clapped her hands at their joyful reaction, and even Isaac's mother seemed to be pleased with the idea. When Mim changed the topic of conversation to a letter she'd received from a cousin, Isaac had trouble focusing on what his aunt was saying. He couldn't help but look at Sadie. He'd never had such an instant connection with someone, not even Rebecca.

Isaac shooed the intimate thoughts from his mind. He wouldn't allow himself to fall for Sadie. His heart loved one woman, Rebecca, and losing her felt like a knife had been stabbed into his chest. He refused to put himself in a position where he might endure heartbreak for a second time in his life. Sadie was a dear friend, though he feared that he'd already started to view her as more.

Chapter Nine

After a vivid sunrise, the grayish-blue haze of a humid August morning draped over Bird-in-Hand, the oppressive sticky air making it difficult for man and beast to rise from slumber. Despite the sticky weather, Isaac and Mim were up and completing their daily chores before the rooster's first crow. The day of the barn raising had arrived, and there was plenty to be done before folks started arriving.

Isaac and his *aentie* had just finished setting up some folding tables to place refreshments on when the first horses and buggies arrived. Isaac helped the male guests unhitch their horses and led them to a nearby fenced-in pasture, while the women followed Mim into the house, where they would work on sewing a quilt until it was time to prepare lunch for the workers. Children played together in several groups, buzzing around Mim's backyard like swarms of honeybees. By nine o'clock, it seemed like every Amish family living in

Bird-in-Hand had arrived, but there was one specific family that Isaac was especially eager to see.

The Stolzfus clan was one of the last families to arrive. When Sadie stepped out of her family's buggy, the sight of her nearly took Isaac's breath away. She wore a green dress, which perfectly matched the color of her eyes. Her thick, golden hair was pulled into a low traditional bun and mostly hidden beneath her *kapp*. Even dressed so plainly, she looked downright lovely.

Isaac dashed to greet them all, taking a moment to shake hands with Sadie's father, Amos, and her mother, Anna. He also greeted Mose, who had brought along his toolbox. Susannah, Sadie's younger sister, bid a quick hello to Isaac before hurrying off to join a group of girls who were giggling among themselves in a tight cluster.

Glad to have a moment alone with Sadie, Isaac glanced down and noticed that she was holding a pie. "Is that an apple pie?" he asked.

Sadie glanced at the pie and shrugged. "It is. I'm a bit *naerfich*. I've never baked anything for a large gathering before." Her shoulders sagged as if in premature defeat. "Hope I don't make a fool of myself when this is served."

It hurt Isaac to see Sadie looking so unsure of herself. She was clearly stepping out of her comfort zone, and although pride was a sin, he couldn't help but feel proud of her for putting more time and effort into a task that she didn't particularly enjoy. Wanting to encourage her, Isaac said, "You put love into everything you do, so how could this pie not be as sweet as you are?"

Sadie's eyes widened as she gazed up at him. She was

about to say something but someone shouted from the barnyard. "*Kumme*, Isaac! Time's a-wasting!"

Isaac's cheeks flushed pink, feeling embarrassed by his words. "I better get to work. We've got half a barn to build," he replied, rubbing his hands together briskly.

"You better hurry to the tables at lunchtime, since I'm sure lots of folks will be clambering to get a piece of this questionable pie," Sadie called after him, her delightful sarcasm causing Isaac to laugh out loud.

"Sadie, *kumme* work on this quilt with us," Anna beckoned to her daughter, motioning for her to join the group.

"I'll be right there," Sadie sighed, resigned to the fact that her place was at the quilting frame, at least for that day. She stood with her nose nearly pressed against one of the windows, watching the sea of men buzz around the frame of the barn's new addition. Some of the bravest fellows even inched along the wooden beams where the roof would soon be built. Though she had been to several barn raisings during her twenty-one years of life, she never ceased to be dazzled by how quickly a structure could be built. In only a few hours, the shape of the building's addition had been erected, nearly tripling the size of the original barn. The chorus of hammers banging wooden pegs into place reminded Sadie of a herd of stampeding horses, and she found all the construction activity to be fascinating.

"I think my oldest *dochder* would rather have a hammer in her hand than a quilting needle," Anna said to no one in particular as she worked on her portion of the quilt, her needle flying effortlessly in and out of the fabric.

"Could be that Sadie would rather spend her day outside watching a certain young man who's working on that barn," Mim replied, peering over her glasses, which rested on the edge of her nose.

Ruth, who was seated beside her sister, peeked up at Sadie, then exchanged knowing glances with Anna and Mim. Sadie thought she spotted the start of a grin forming on Ruth's lips, but it quickly faded away. A few muffled chuckles escaped from some of the other ladies seated around the quilting frame.

"I know when I'm being teased, and I don't like it one bit," Sadie declared, planting her hands on her hips. She tried her best to muster a serious face, but she couldn't hide the smile that felt like it was bursting through. Truthfully, she enjoyed the lighthearted banter from the dear women in this community, and she was glad to be part of a church family that cared for her.

"*Ach*, it's a *mamm*'s job to tease her *dochder*, and keep her nose in her *kinner*'s business," Anna replied, looking up from her sewing to give her daughter a wink. "Why don't you sit yourself down and work on this quilt with us?"

Though she could quickly think of dozens of other things that she would rather do instead of quilting, Sadie forced herself over to the quilting frame and took a seat between her mother and Ruth. After Ruth handed her some thread and a needle, and her mother explained the portion of the quilt that they had been assigned to, Sadie set to work, doing her best to sew neat, even stitches.

"Speaking of that special man," Anna continued,

"I've noticed some changes in you ever since you and Isaac started courting."

"Like what?" Sadie asked, focusing so much on her stitching that she forgot to blink, causing her eyes to burn.

"You've always been my sweet, happy *maedel*, ever since you were little. But since you've been spending time with Isaac, I've noticed that you've been even more chipper." Anna giggled quietly, looking up from her sewing to grin at her daughter. "Can't remember a time when you've had a constant smile on your face from sunup 'til sundown."

"*Jah*, your *mamm*'s right," Mim agreed as she snipped a piece of thread. "You fairly glow, Sadie. Just between us," she said, lowering her voice as she leaned closer to her young friend, "Isaac's had a real spring in his step lately as well."

Sadie bit the inside of her cheek to keep from squealing. "Really?"

"*Ach*, of course! I mean, I haven't spent this much time with him since I visited my sister's family in Indiana over ten years ago. I can only speak for the time he's been living here in Bird-in-Hand, but he does seem to smile an awful lot on days when he spends time with you. Wouldn't you agree, Ruth?" Isaac's mother bobbed her head enthusiastically, but of course, she made no verbal reply.

The topic of conversation soon changed to a new fabric shop that would soon be opening in the neighboring town of Strasburg, but Sadie had difficulty concentrating on that, or any of the countless conversations happening around the quilting frame. Instead, she found herself tickled pink from hearing Mim's description of the effect she'd had on Isaac. She couldn't deny it: they made a great pair, and a connection like theirs was so rarely found.

A hint of gloominess dimmed the sunshine of this revelation. Eventually, Sadie and Isaac would end their courtship of convenience. That would mean spending a lot less time together, and that was something Sadie didn't want to think about. She shoved the idea out of her mind and focused even more intently on her quilting stitches, determined to enjoy this day of fellowship with her church family, as well as her courtship with Isaac, even if was to be short-lived.

"Would you hand me another board instead of just standing there and smiling?"

Isaac's daydream was interrupted by Mose's request. "*Jah, jah*, sorry about that," he replied, reaching for a board from the pile of planks. He handed the board up to Mose, who was balanced on a nearby ladder.

Mose chuckled as he hammered the plank into place. "I've seen that dopey look on my own face recently." He motioned for Isaac to hand him another plank. "Saw it whenever I looked in the mirror after I started courting Rhoda."

Isaac snickered at Mose's observation, then was startled by its implications. Why would he have a lovestruck grin on his face if he were merely courting Sadie to avoid a proper courtship? Sure, he enjoyed her company and admired her unique personality, but certainly, that was the extent of it. Still, Isaac wondered how Sadie had managed to remain single throughout her courting years, and he voiced that very question to Mose.

"Well," Mose began as he climbed down the ladder, "when we were *kinner*, Sadie was kind of a tomboy. She preferred the rough-and-tumble games we would play during recess at our schoolhouse instead of playing with her faceless doll with the other *maedels*." He picked up his jug of water, which was resting in the shade, and took a long drink. "As she got older, her interests began to include bird-watching, fishing, gardening and really anything else that got her outside. The other *maedels* were busy attending quilting bees and trying to outdo each other's newfound baking skills. I guess folks thought it was odd that Sadie would rather spend time in nature than doing things that the others were doing."

Isaac wiped away some sweat from the back of his neck. The blazing sun was growing hotter by the minute, and he hoped that it would soon be time to have lunch and rest in the shade for an hour or so. "So the fellows around here overlooked her just for being different?"

Mose nodded as he took another swig of water. "*Jah*, but I suppose there might be some men who are intimidated by a strong, independent woman like my twin." His expression hardened as if he was recalling a painful memory. "When we first started attending the young people's gatherings several years ago, one of the more immature fellows sent a letter to Sadie, asking if he could be her date and give her a ride home in his courting buggy. Sadie buzzed with excitement that whole week leading up to the singing, only to watch the fellow leave the event with another *maedel*. It was some sort of cruel practical joke."

Isaac frowned, filling with anger at the thought of someone intentionally hurting someone as sweet as Sadie. "That's *baremlich*!"

"*Jah*, but it caused Sadie to have a revelation about what she wanted in life. After that night, she told me that she couldn't see the point of courting unless she felt a genuine connection with a fellow." Mose smiled and slapped Isaac on the back before ascending the ladder. "That means you must be awful special, or at least my sister thinks so."

Before Isaac could reply, the clanging sound of Mim's supper bell rang out through the air. The dozens of men who had been working on the barn scrambled to put their tools away before making their way toward the long folding tables that held the noon meal. As he made his way toward the feast, Mose's words flitted around Isaac's mind. It did something to his heart to know that Sadie found him to be someone special. What was it about him that made him worthy of such a unique, sweet woman's affection?

When Isaac saw Sadie exiting Mim's house, smiling and laughing with the other women as they brought pitchers of lemonade to the tables, Isaac had to look away from her. What nonsense it was to entertain the idea that Sadie might view him as anything more than a friend. Their courtship was merely a mutually beneficial solution to their temporary problems. He would need to be sure to remind himself of that fact regularly, lest his mind start to wonder about the possibility of finding love for the second time in his life.

Chapter Ten

By the time the sun had set, the exterior of the addition was completed and painted white to match the existing portion of Mim's barn. The majority of the families in attendance had departed once the job was complete, but the Stolzfus family remained, and all but one of them were relaxing on Mim's porch, enjoying some of her famous gingersnap cookies.

After the productive, physically exhausting day, Isaac was glad to finally enjoy some quiet time with Sadie as he gave her a tour of the work that had been completed that day. They ambled around the structure several times, both of them pointing out the fine craftsmanship of the building. As they headed inside the barn's addition, Isaac held the gas lantern out to light their way. "The interior still needs some work, but I'll be able to do that over the winter months. I'm not one to brag, but I think we did a pretty nice job getting this barn expanded."

Sadie looked up toward the rafters and watched as a

barn swallow happily assessed its new home. "I agree, and so does that little critter."

Isaac chuckled as he handed Sadie the lantern. He sprinted across the massive room to a bale of hay. He easily lifted the square bale and brought it over to Sadie, then motioned for her to take a seat. "*Jah*, I had a right nice day getting this addition built. How was your day?"

Sadie plopped down onto the hay bale. "It was nice to spend some time with our church family outside of a Sunday service." She paused while Isaac hurried across the vast room and brought over a second hay bale to use as a seat for himself. "We were working on a log cabin wedding quilt to give Leah Beiler as a gift since she and Daniel are getting married in November. It was kind of an inside joke, though, since Leah was also working on the quilt, but she didn't know that someday it will be hers."

Isaac pushed his hay bale next to Sadie's and then took a seat. "I think she'll like that."

Sadie nodded as she leaned forward and placed the lantern on the floor several feet in front of them. "It was Nancy's idea and she organized everything. It was nice of her, even though she chose not to speak to me," Sadie said with a smirk and a wink, showing that she wasn't truly bothered by Nancy's snubbing.

"*Ach*, she always has a bee in her bonnet." Isaac guffawed, glad that Sadie didn't take nonsense like that to heart.

"I think she's jealous that we're courting," Sadie replied, quirking one of her sandy eyebrows.

"Well, she can pout all she wants, because I'm all

yours." Isaac grinned, quickly feeling his face flush with heat. Hopefully, Sadie had taken what he'd said as only a joke and not something more. Deciding it was best to change the subject, he declared, "That apple pie you brought was downright tasty."

Sadie's green eyes squinted in the low light of the gas lantern. "There were eggshells in it. I didn't realize I'd accidentally mixed them in with the apples until I cut the first slice to be served."

Isaac shrugged. "So? It was still tasty. A little crunch never hurt anyone."

Sadie stared at Isaac for a few moments, then let loose with a laugh that bounced around the barn. Her giggles caused Isaac to chuckle, and soon the pair were nearly doubled over in laughter. Once they composed themselves, Sadie wiped a tear from her eye and swept her gaze around the empty barn once more. "I'm glad that Mim agreed to add on to her old stable. Now you'll have the space you need to start farming next year."

Isaac rubbed a knot in his sore shoulder, his muscles tired from hours of hammering, lifting and climbing. "I sure would love to farm for Mim, but who knows how long *Mamm* and I will be staying here. Can't set up to farm if I'm just going to abandon it when I return to Indiana."

Sadie's posture slumped a bit. She pulled a piece of hay from the bale and began twirling it between her fingers. "Would you ever consider permanently moving to Bird-in-Hand?"

Isaac let out a long sigh and stood, then started pacing circles around the two hay bales. Moving permanently to Lancaster County and finally dedicating his life to farming felt like a dream that could never be fulfilled. "I wish I could, but if our prayers are answered and *Mamm* recovers, we'll be headed back to Indiana. That's my home, and there's no reason for me to move just to farm when I already have a job at my *daed*'s woodworking shop."

Sadie's eyes grew as wide as a harvest moon. Her mouth fell open slightly as she looked up at him before dropping her gaze to the ground. She released the piece of hay that she had been fiddling with and folded her hands in her lap. "There's nothing for you here in Pennsylvania?"

Thrown off by Sadie's sudden change in disposition, Isaac wondered if he'd said the wrong thing. Had he accidentally insinuated that she meant nothing to him?

Before Isaac could tell her that he'd misspoken, Susannah rushed into the barn, slightly out of breath. "Been looking for you all over, Sadie! *Daed* says it's time to head home."

"*Jah*, okay, I'll be right there," Sadie replied solemnly. Susannah nodded and darted out of the barn just as quickly as she had arrived. Sadie glanced briefly at Isaac, as if she was unwilling to look him in the eye. "I'll see you later." She hurried out of the barn and into the evening's fresh air.

Isaac could have slapped himself in the face. "Me and my big mouth," he muttered, giving one of the hay bales a good kick. He hoped that he hadn't damaged his friendship with Sadie, and now he'd have to wait until another day to find out if he had.

* * *

Just after ten o'clock that night, Sadie tiptoed noise-lessly around her second-floor bedroom, eager for the day to come to an end. She pulled on her flowing white nightgown, glad to slip into the comfortable attire. Letting down her waist-length locks from her low bun, Sadie sat on the edge of her bed, brushing out the tangles. With each brushstroke came a new memory of the evening's disappointing turn of events, letting Sadie know that a long, sleepless night lay before her.

After escaping her disheartening conversation with Isaac in the newly built barn, Sadie was quiet for the rest of the evening. When questioned by both Susannah and her parents on the short buggy ride home, she had been in no mood to discuss what had made her usually bright smile disappear. "My stomach is awful upset" was the excuse she'd half-heartedly given them. It wasn't a lie. She'd felt queasy ever since Isaac had admitted that their courtship meant nothing to him. It deeply confused and frustrated her as to why this bothered her so intensely. After all, they were only friends who had agreed to court for appearance's sake. So why did she feel her heart sink to the pit of her stomach when Isaac had only stated the obvious?

Once the family buggy arrived home, Sadie had wandered deep into the nearby towering cornstalks. She wept in the privacy of the country skyscrapers, watering the soil with a deluge of tears. When she felt she had no more left to cry, she'd crept back to the house and up the stairs to her bedroom, where she'd spent the next several hours avoiding her family's questioning glances.

As she finished thoroughly brushing her golden hair, Sadie heard a quiet conversation coming from her parents' adjacent bedroom. Out of habit, she'd left her bedroom door ajar, lest the room become too stuffy on that late summer night. She stood to close the door, wanting to avoid unconsciously eavesdropping. However, what she heard her father say next caused her to stop in her tracks.

"I imagine we'll be busy planning a wedding pretty soon."

Sadie's heart skipped a beat at the notion. Mose must have said something to their father to hint that he was planning on marrying Rhoda in November's wedding season. As their parents' only son, Mose was a big help to their father when it came to all the daily farm chores. If Mose mentioned his plans to wed Rhoda in the near future, he was likely doing so to politely prepare their father for the fact that he might soon need to hire some additional help once Mose had moved out of the house.

Although Sadie would miss having her twin nearby, she wondered if she might be asked to help out with the farm chores and outdoor work. "And what a *wunderbar* blessing it will be, to have Rhoda as my sister-in-law," Sadie whispered to herself, instantly forgetting about her sadness. With a joyful wedding on the horizon and the possibility of getting outdoors more often, Sadie felt her spirits start to perk up.

"*Ach*, Amos!" Sadie's mother's sweet voice gently scolded her husband, though she didn't sound truly peeved. "I didn't think we'd be seeing one of our *kinner* leave the nest so soon!"

Her father chuckled. "Nothing to worry yourself over. Our *dochders* will still be here even after Mose becomes a married man."

"*Jah*, though I worry about our Sadie sometimes." *Mamm*'s tone had changed dramatically, now sounding full of concern and pity.

There was a long pause before *Daed* spoke again. "I do too. Until recently, I feared that she'd spend her life alone once her siblings were married and you and I have gone home to glory. But since that Isaac fellow has taken an interest in her, it gives me hope that she'll have a family of her own, whether or not Isaac is the man she chooses in the end."

Her father's implication was as clear as a freshly washed windowpane. He expected that Sadie would remain forever unmarried, never to share her life with someone she loved. The weight of his unintentional blow nearly knocked the wind out of Sadie. She stood motionless, feeling tears roll down her cheeks as her suspicions were once again confirmed. People assumed that she was destined to become an old maid, and even her own parents seemed convinced that her future was to be a lonely one. To make matters worse, Isaac wasn't even her real beau. He was merely a close friend, nothing more.

Sadie lightly walked closer to her bedroom door, holding her breath to ensure that her parents would not hear her sniffles. Once she closed the door, she wandered back to her bed, which was draped with a handmade purple, pink and white quilt, stitched together in a patchwork design. Sadie turned off her lantern, collapsed onto her bed and slipped under her quilt, wishing that the comfortable bed would swallow her up.

As she rolled onto her side and pulled her knees up to her chest, Sadie covered her mouth to muffle her sobs. She had never been able to picture herself falling in love and raising a houseful of children, since that would require finding a mate who would accept her quirkiness, but knowing that even *Mamm* and *Daed* seemed to share those thoughts ripped Sadie's heart to shreds. Was it true? Would she never find love?

Memories of the eve of her sixteenth birthday drifted into Sadie's mind. That special night had been the first time that she had attended a singing. Full of girlish excitement and hope for the future, teenage Sadie had taken it in stride when not one fellow looked her way or offered to give her a ride home. Unfortunately for her, being overlooked while her friends found love soon became a noticeable trend. At the point where Sadie had given up on finding her soul mate, both Isaac and her parents had confirmed her worst fear, that she'd likely spend all of her days without someone to call her own.

Clutching her pillow as if it were her only friend in the world, Sadie continued to cry until her pillowcase was thoroughly damp. Flipping it over to the dry side, Sadie considered spilling her aching heart to the Lord and asking Him to soothe her broken spirit. Emotionally exhausted and deciding all hope was lost, Sadie nixed the idea and cried until she drifted into a fitful sleep.

Chapter Eleven

Isaac sat at the workbench in a sunny corner of Mim's barn, realizing how very quiet the past week had been. Even though the cows were grazing contentedly in a nearby pasture, and Shadow and Mim's mare, Daisy, playfully chased each other back and forth across the meadow, things seemed to be unusually still. Even the barn swallows, who normally swooped in and out of the barn dozens of times each day, were absent from their nests high in the rafters.

"No wonder it seems so dull around here," Isaac muttered to himself as he stared at the tools hung neatly on the wall before him. A week had passed since the barn raising, and since his last conversation with Sadie. Isaac had spent the entire time worrying about the status of their relationship. After he'd mentioned his eventual plans to return to Indiana, Sadie's typically bubbly demeanor had visibly darkened. She'd looked pained, and for the life of him, Isaac couldn't fully understand why. Friends often had to say goodbye to each other

Treat Yourself with 2 Free Books!

Romance

Suspense

GET UP TO 4 FREE BOOKS & 2 FREE GIFTS WORTH OVER $20

See Inside For Details

Claim Them While You Can

Get ready to relax and indulge with your FREE BOOKS and more!

Claim up to FOUR NEW BOOKS & TWO MYSTERY GIFTS – absolutely FREE!

Dear Reader,

We both know life can be difficult at times. That's why it's important to treat yourself so you can relax and recharge once in a while.

And I'd like to help you do this by sending you this amazing offer of up to FOUR brand new full length FREE BOOKS that WE pay for.

This is everything I have ready to send to you right now:

Try **Love Inspired® Romance Larger-Print** books and fall in love with inspirational romances that take you on an uplifting journey of faith, forgiveness and hope.

Try **Love Inspired® Suspense Larger-Print** books where courage and optimism unite in stories of faith and love in the face of danger.

Or **TRY BOTH!**

All we ask in return is that you answer 4 simple questions on the attached Treat Yourself survey. You'll get **Two Free Books** and **Two Mystery Gifts** from each series you try, *altogether worth over $20*! Who could pass up a deal like that?

Sincerely,

Pam Powers

Harlequin Reader Service

Treat Yourself to Free Books and Free Gifts.

Answer 4 fun questions and get rewarded.

**We love to connect with our readers!
Please tell us a little about you...**

◄ DETACH AND MAIL CARD TODAY! ▼

	YES	NO
1. I LOVE reading a good book.	○	○
2. I indulge and "treat" myself often.	○	○
3. I love getting FREE things.	○	○
4. Reading is one of my favorite activities.	○	

TREAT YOURSELF • Pick your 2 Free Books...

Yes! Please send me my Free Books from each series I select and Free Mystery Gifts. I understand that I am under no obligation to buy anything, as explained on the back of this card.

Which do you prefer?

❏ **Love Inspired® Romance Larger-Print** 122/322 IDL GRDP
❏ **Love Inspired® Suspense Larger-Print** 107/307 IDL GRDP
❏ **Try Both** 122/322 & 107/307 IDL GRED

FIRST NAME   LAST NAME

ADDRESS

APT.#   CITY

STATE/PROV.   ZIP/POSTAL CODE

EMAIL ❏ Please check this box if you would like to receive newsletters and promotional emails from Harlequin Enterprises ULC and its affiliates. You can unsubscribe anytime.

LI/SLI-520-TY22

and ® are trademarks owned by Harlequin Enterprises ULC. Printed in the U.S.A.

If offer card is missing write to: Harlequin Reader Service, P.O. Box 1341, Buffalo, NY 14240-8531 or visit www.ReaderService.com

BUSINESS REPLY MAIL
FIRST-CLASS MAIL   PERMIT NO. 717   BUFFALO, NY

POSTAGE WILL BE PAID BY ADDRESSEE

HARLEQUIN READER SERVICE
PO BOX 1341
BUFFALO NY 14240-8571

NO POSTAGE
NECESSARY
IF MAILED
IN THE
UNITED STATES

when one of them moved away, and that was a fact of life. Their relationship was a bit more complex than a simple friendship, Isaac reminded himself, knowing that he wanted Sadie to be a permanent part of his life.

Should he go over to her house to see if she was truly upset with him? Arriving unannounced at her home might make things worse. Besides, if Sadie had told Mose that Isaac had upset her, her protective twin brother might not be too happy to see him either. Had he ruined their friendship just by being honest about how he saw the future unfolding?

"Isaac?" Mim called out as she rounded the corner with a full pitcher in one hand and a basket handle hanging in the crook of her other arm. "Whatcha doing out here?"

Isaac cleared his throat and faked a smile, unwilling to admit that he'd spent the last few hours moping around, unsure of what to do. "I was just taking a break."

"Perfect timing, then," Mim chirped as she set the basket and pitcher down on the workbench. "Figured I'd bring your lunch out here when you didn't come inside. I rang the supper bell three times, you know."

Now that his aunt had appeared with her picnic basket, Isaac realized that his hunger pains were nearly as intense as his worry over Sadie. He eagerly reached into the basket to see what Mim had brought him, and was pleased to find a turkey and cheese sandwich, homemade potato chips and a red velvet whoopie pie. He thanked her for the meal, then bowed his head in prayer before ravenously biting into the sandwich.

"Your *mamm* has regressed a bit recently," Mim somberly mentioned to Isaac as she watched him devour his sandwich. "Seems like Sadie was the only one able to perk her up." Mim's expression brightened with an unmistakable blush of hope. "She used to come over a few times a week to visit either you or your *mamm*, but she hasn't come around since the barn raising. Will Sadie be visiting again, you think?"

Isaac frowned so hard that his face ached, feeling as if he was being interrogated. "How would I know what Sadie plans to do?"

Mim's brow rose at Isaac's sour tone. "I thought you two were a courting couple, but of course it's none of my business." She reached for a nearby broom and used it to sweep away a large cobweb from the corner. "Your *mamm* isn't the only one in better spirits when Sadie stops by."

Determined to respect his elder, Isaac bit his tongue instead of bickering with his aunt. He sighed and ran a hand through his straw-colored hair, ruffling it up as if he'd just walked through a storm. "Sadie and I had a talk the day of the barn raising, and it didn't go so well."

Mim spun around, leaning the broom against the wall before hurrying back to the workbench, where her nephew sat. "Want to talk about it?" she asked, ignoring the broom when it slowly slid to one side before falling over.

Truthfully, Isaac didn't want to discuss this private matter with anyone. But considering that the Lord might have nudged Mim to ask about Sadie so that she could share some wisdom and advice, Isaac decided to share the concerns that had been plaguing him. "We got to talking about the future, and I mentioned that I would head back to Indiana should *Mamm* recover." He paused, somewhat embarrassed. "I said that there was nothing keeping me here in Bird-in-Hand, so it wouldn't make sense for me to move here permanently."

Mim nodded ever so slightly. "And Sadie got upset with you?"

"Well, she didn't come right out and say that, but it sure seemed like what I said bothered her."

"It's clear that Sadie cares for you, Isaac. Could be that your statement gave her the impression that your connection with her isn't strong enough to keep you in Lancaster County," Mim suggested as she reached down to pick up a friendly gray barn cat that had approached.

Isaac stared at the whoopie pie in the basket, though his appetite had left him. "I didn't mean to imply that I didn't value our friendship, because that's not true at all."

Mim stroked the barn cat as it cuddled close to her chest. "Friendship? Is that all you have with Sadie?"

Isaac's gaze dropped to the floor as Mim's question struck a chord deep within him. "It's complicated," he said so quietly that he barely heard his own reply.

Mim placed the cat back on the ground. "There's nothing complicated about two hearts that belong together." She smiled at the cat, then at her nephew. "Why don't you go pay Sadie a visit, after you finish your lunch, that is." She eyed his half-eaten sandwich and gave him the glare of a strict parent.

While Isaac was sure that Mim was mistaken about

the possibility of a romantic future between him and Sadie, he agreed that they needed to have a heart-to-heart conversation. Deciding that he would go to the greenhouse after lunch, Isaac sent up a quick prayer that Sadie would be willing to talk to him.

Sadie hadn't been able to shake the sadness that had loomed over her since her last conversation with Isaac until it was time for her to work at the greenhouse. Being among the flowers and plants felt like a balm to her aching heart. What a blessing it was to know that *Gott* had ordained her to look after some of His artistry, nourishing it and helping it to grow, before passing on His creation to others.

Caring for the colorful mums and asters helped to cheer her up. She sang quietly to herself as she spent her morning watering both the indoor and outdoor plants. She answered the occasional question from customers and also put out some food for the greenhouse cat, Whiskers, who was somewhat of a mascot for the store. Before her lunch break, she swept the cement floor of the greenhouse, creating a small pile of dead leaves, soil and pebbles. She took pride in keeping both the shop and the attached greenhouse spick-and-span, and even the mundane task was something she found joy in doing.

When she bent to sweep the collected rubbish into a dustpan, she heard a man's voice calling her name. Then came the racket of a clumsy clattering, as if a bull had charged into a china cabinet. Startled, Sadie straightened to her full height and was amused to see Isaac steadying the large display of seed packets that he must have collided with. Several packets fluttered to the ground like autumn leaves on a breezy day. Red-faced, Isaac immediately bent to pick them up.

"Well, you've certainly caught my attention," Sadie laughed as she walked toward the calamity. Even though there was some lingering pain caused by their last interaction, Sadie couldn't deny that she was pleased and somewhat relieved to see Isaac. She hadn't felt whole for the past several days, and seeing Isaac now felt like a missing puzzle piece had returned to her life.

"Sorry," Isaac muttered. "I suppose this is the second dumb thing I've done recently."

"*Ach*, don't say that," Sadie said with encouragement as she helped Isaac collect some of the packets. "Maybe you've just invented a new way to plant seeds." She offered him a sympathetic smile, displeased to hear him speak poorly of himself. "What's got you so flustered?"

As if unable to look her in the eye, Isaac stared at the cluster of packets he'd picked up as he handed them to Sadie. "I guess I'm just a bit *naerfich*. I've been thinking a lot about the last conversation we had, and I thought we needed to have a talk about it."

Sadie accepted the seed packets from Isaac, placing each one into its correct slot on the display. "I've been thinking about that night too," she admitted, hoping Isaac hadn't noticed the crack in her voice.

Isaac glanced around the greenhouse before focusing on Sadie. "I'll just come right out and say it." His posture straightened as if he was putting on the bravest front that he could muster. "Saying that I had nothing keeping me in Lancaster County was a poor choice of words. I think you might have taken that to mean that our friendship...our relationship...isn't worth moving for, and that is far from the truth." Isaac reached for Sadie's hand and held it securely, his coffee-colored eyes gazing directly into hers. "You mean the world to me, Sadie. Truly, you do. I'll do my best to show you how much I treasure you."

"*Jah*, you mean an awful lot to me as well," Sadie replied, feeling as if she was nearly floating. Isaac's sentimental words and the touch of his hand holding hers caused Sadie to experience a rush of emotions that she hadn't expected. There was no denying it now. She was developing feelings for the man she was courting for the sake of convenience. Sadie tried to convince herself not to pine over a man who would never be truly hers, even if Isaac was the kindest, most understanding, handsome man she'd ever met.

"Now that this has been put behind us, why don't you show me around the greenhouse?" Isaac suggested as he let go of Sadie's hand. "I've been curious to see this place since you've told me so much about it."

"*Jah*, of course." She bobbed her head, leading the way as they walked through the property. Truly in her element, Sadie beamed as she showed Isaac the hardy plants that would soon be available for the upcoming autumn sale. The vibrant yellow, orange, pink and purple mums were her favorites, and Isaac agreed that he was partial to them as well. She couldn't help but notice Isaac smiling attentively at her as she explained the different varieties of houseplants. As they neared the front of the store, Isaac stopped to look at some bird feeders that were for sale, then decided to purchase one with some seed.

After Isaac paid for his items, he and Sadie walked to the parking lot, where his horse and buggy were tied to the hitching rail. They continued their pleasant conversation while Isaac loaded his purchases into the back of his buggy. "There's gonna be a singing at the Beiler farm next Saturday. Would you like to go?"

"*Jah*, I would," Sadie eagerly replied, glad that things had been worked out between her and Isaac, at least for the time being.

"*Gut*, since there is no one else I'd rather attend with," Isaac responded with a cheesy grin and a comical tip of his hat.

Sadie chuckled as he climbed into his buggy and then waved as the rig pulled out of the greenhouse's parking lot. Once Isaac had safely guided the horse onto the quiet lane, Sadie turned to head back into the greenhouse with some added pep in her step. Though she would need to work hard to keep her growing romantic interest in Isaac at bay, she looked forward to the upcoming gathering. If things continued the way they were going, she and Isaac would certainly grow even closer, and that was something that Sadie desired more than anything else.

Chapter Twelve

When the Saturday of the singing arrived, Isaac could have floated up to the moon with excitement. For the past several days his mind had been filled with thoughts of Sadie, and he knew that this outing would satisfy his growing need to be near her. There was something about her sweet nature, unique personality and lovely smile that drew him to her, and he knew that they were in for a special evening together.

Presently, as he sat at a long folding table in the Beilers' barn with some of his male peers, Isaac glanced nonchalantly in Sadie's direction. As was typical, since courting couples didn't pair off until later in the evening, she'd spent most of the Saturday-night youth gathering socializing with her friends and was now seated at a nearby table, sharing a slice of pie with Rhoda and Leah.

Isaac watched the group of girls as they giggled among themselves. He had spent his time playing cornerball with the other young men, singing fast-paced songs with the large group and eating his fill of baked goods, which provided hours of entertaining fellowship. But now, as things started to wind down, he was faced with a conundrum. Soon the time would come to steal Sadie away from her friends. But then what? Isaac pondered, tuning out the friendly debate between the *youngies* seated at his table.

Normally a young man would take his sweetheart out riding late into the night hours before returning her safely home. Would Sadie expect him to take her out riding? Isaac reached under his hat to scratch his head, realizing that engaging in a courtship for appearance's sake came with unexpected complications. Not that he would mind spending some extra time with Sadie tonight, Isaac pleasantly admitted to himself. She was always good company and a balm for the soul.

Isaac rose from his seat, said a quick goodbye to his friends and headed toward Sadie. Though the singing wasn't over and dusk hadn't yet turned to night, Isaac was eager to check in with her. As he approached the group of smiling ladies, Isaac's confidence suddenly left him. Why was he feeling nervous around Sadie? They were friends, after all. Yet Isaac still felt his pulse increase and heat rush to his face as he neared the table where Sadie was seated.

Full of self-doubt, Isaac stopped when he reached the cluster of girls. They were so absorbed in their conversation that none of them immediately noticed his presence. He reached out to tap Sadie's shoulder, but quickly pulled his hand back. Instead, he quietly cleared his throat in hope of capturing her attention.

Sadie turned, and her already smiling face brightened like sunshine. "Hi, Isaac! Wanna go for a walk with me?"

"*Jah*, s-sure." Isaac stumbled over his words, surprised that Sadie had beaten him to the punch. Could it be that she was eager to spend some one-on-one time with him as well? The possibility warmed his heart. Isaac smiled and nodded at Rhoda and Leah. Sadie's friends returned the gesture and then shot knowing, teasing glances in Sadie's direction. Sadie took the gentle banter in stride as she stood and pushed in her chair, with her nose high in the air. Her haughty attitude was clearly a farce that she couldn't maintain. Sadie giggled, wished her friends a good night and followed Isaac out of the Beilers' barn.

As they stepped into the twilight and away from the crowded barn, Isaac felt free to speak. "Your friends seemed amused when I stole you away. I hope they don't hold that against me, since it's still early in the evening."

Sadie shook her head vehemently. "They're just glad to see that I found myself a nice beau." She smiled up at him before quickly glancing away, her cheeks blushing a pretty shade of rose.

Isaac stared down at the path that led from the barn to the buggy shed, where dozens of open courting rigs stood parked, waiting for their owners to return with their dates. Then he released a concerned sigh. "Did you tell them the truth about our courtship?"

Sadie shook her head again, causing her *kapp*'s ribbons to flutter. "No one knows the truth." As they continued to walk, she wrapped her arms around her middle, as if protecting herself.

They strolled beside the wooden fence that twisted

throughout the Beilers' rolling land. As they walked together beneath a soft orange-and-pink sunset, Isaac listened intently as Sadie told him more about her parents and siblings, as well as her adventure-filled girlhood days. Sadie seemed equally intrigued when Isaac shared details about his gaggle of sisters and his father's woodworking shop in Indiana. Isaac shared more about how he hadn't met Aunt Miriam until he was nearly ten years old. That was the year Mim had traveled to Indiana to visit her sister's family. Though he was aware that Mim's storytelling abilities drew the attention of many local children, Isaac found it charming when Sadie fondly recounted her own childhood memories of spending time with his aunt to hear her tales and eat her cookies.

Lost in pleasant conversation, Isaac and Sadie traveled quite a distance and soon wandered into one of the meadows. A strong scent of fresh-cut grass perfumed the air, as it often did when animals had spent time grazing there. The fragrance seemed nearly nostalgic and filled with comfort as Isaac breathed in the scent with contentment. When was the last time he had stopped to smell the proverbial roses? Certainly not since Rebecca had passed away.

Isaac turned to Sadie to comment on this revelation and was surprised to see that she was no longer at his side. He spun around and was stunned to see Sadie on her hands and knees, her nose pressed into the grass. "Sadie! *Was iss letz?*"

Sadie tilted her head up toward Isaac while remaining on the ground. "Nothing's wrong. I'm just smelling the grass. Grass is a plant, too, you know, and I think every plant should be enjoyed." With this explanation, Sadie promptly returned her nose to the earth.

Amused by her odd behavior, Isaac's mouth dropped open. "And you crawl on the ground to do that?"

"Well, sure! That's where the scent is best." Sadie loudly inhaled through her nose several times, then finally stood. She shook some loose strands of grass from her dress and wiped her palms on her apron. "We have to savor it while we can, ain't so? Autumn will soon be knocking on the door, and then it'll be months before we smell something so fresh again."

Isaac stared at Sadie with his mouth agape as she stared back at him. It was a ridiculous but intelligent, strange but honest, explanation. Sadie's pure outlook on life was enough to light a fire in even the coldest heart.

"What?" Sadie leaned her head to the side as if she genuinely didn't understand Isaac's astonishment.

Isaac grinned from ear to ear, taking in the beautiful sight before him. As the sun set behind her, its vibrant yellow rays lined perfectly behind Sadie's sheer, organdy *kapp*. The glow around her head covering appeared almost like a halo, highlighting both her inner and outer beauty.

"What are you staring at?"

Sadie's voice interrupted Isaac's growing admiration for her. He grinned, deciding to tell her exactly what was on his mind. "I was just thinking that you're as lovely as a field full of wildflowers."

"Puh," Sadie exclaimed with a wave of her hand. "I don't know about that, but I might have inhaled a flower or two," she replied as she rubbed the tip of her nose.

Isaac burst into a fit of laughter at Sadie's objection.

Sadie gawked at him as if he'd lost his mind, which made him whoop and roar all the more. Eventually, Sadie joined in the uproar with a few cackles of her own.

"Speaking of funny things," Isaac managed to say once he'd regained his composure, "was it kinda awkward being here tonight?"

Sadie sprinted forward to catch up with Isaac, and the pair began walking side by side once again. "What do you mean?"

Isaac felt a strong, thick weed snap beneath his boot. "I guess it just felt weird being in Nancy's territory with my *aldi*." Referring to Sadie as his girlfriend sounded strangely natural, which alarmed Isaac a bit. Pushing the sensation out of his mind, he continued, "I'm thrilled to have avoided getting tangled up with Nancy, but I didn't realize it was a blessing in disguise. It brought me to the dearest friend I've ever had, and I don't know what I'd do without you in my life."

Sadie stopped walking and reached for Isaac's hand, halting his pace as well. "That is the nicest thing anyone has ever said to me." She leaned closer to Isaac and lowered her voice, though not a soul was near enough to hear their conversation. "You have a good heart, Isaac. People see that. I see that, and the Lord does too."

Sadie had a way of looking through a person, past their pain, and their defenses. In the short time that they had known each other, she truly saw Isaac for who he was and had unveiled a secret he was trying to hide from even himself. Losing his only love to a tragic death had been horrendous. His mother's emotional breakdown following the incident was morbid. Two years ago, he'd decided to move on with his life, yet he'd done so without hope. But Sadie's presence in his life had reawakened his hibernating sense of hope. Effortlessly, she had planted a seed in the barren wasteland of Isaac's spirit. As that tiny, hopeful seedling began to sprout, Sadie watered it with wisdom and warmed it with kindness.

Isaac opened his mouth to share his epiphany with Sadie, but before he could utter a word, Sadie darted away. She ran a few steps, gently clapped and stopped. Unsure of what Sadie was up to this time, Isaac watched as she lunged forward again. Then he noticed a tiny flash of neon green, which Sadie delicately captured in cupped hands. She was chasing fireflies.

Now that she had gently trapped the shining bug, Sadie hurried back to Isaac. "Put your hands out," Sadie said softly so as to not startle the living light bulb. Amused, Isaac presented his outstretched palms and stood as still as a frozen creek while the summer insect crept from Sadie's hands into his.

"Look how special this lightning bug is." Sadie leaned in for a closer look as the intermittent green glow illuminated her face. "These little ones are only with us for the summer. These are probably the last ones of the season, with the cooler weather soon coming." She straightened to her full height and continued to watch the firefly. A few seconds passed before the insect flew away, and Sadie's eyes met Isaac's. "We can always count on the Lord to send us a little light. We need only look for it, *jah*?"

"*Jah*, and tonight He certainly sent me two little lights."

"I hope you're not referring to me, because I'm too big to catch!" Sadie threw her head back with a laugh, then scampered off to hunt for more lightning bugs.

Feeling as if he were alive for the first time since Rebecca's death, Isaac dropped the weight of the melancholy that he had carried for the past two years. He shook free from the shackles of hopelessness that he hadn't realized had chained him down, then joined in the firefly hunt. Living fully in the simplicity and delight of the moment, he felt as if several cinder blocks had been removed from his spirit.

Like schoolchildren, Isaac and Sadie romped through the meadows until it was nearly too dark to see. Laughing as they nearly collided several times, they captured lightning bugs on a catch-and-release basis, marveling at their sparkling surroundings. Darkness snuck up on the unlikely pair but wasn't noticed until they stopped their frolicking to catch their breath. Sadie dramatically collapsed into the grass as if she'd just run clear across Lancaster County. When she landed with a thud, puffs of dandelion seedlings flew into the air, along with several additional lightning bugs.

Isaac took a seat on the ground next to Sadie, chuckling at her shenanigans. "I haven't had fun like this in…I don't know how long."

With her back pressed against the ground, Sadie stared up at the bright full moon. "Who would've thought that a tiny lightning bug could've brought that out of you."

"Jah," Isaac responded, knowing in his heart that it wasn't the firefly that had prompted his breakthrough. "I wonder what time it is. Seems like it got dark real fast."

"'September is here. It's harvest at last. Leaves start a-changing and nighttime comes fast.'" Sadie giggled after reciting her limerick. "Well, at least, it will be September soon."

Isaac glanced at Sadie and let out a little laugh. "What's that?"

Sadie sat up, resting on her elbows. "My *grossdaddi* says that every year when the days start growing shorter. He's chock-full of little poems like that one."

Isaac bobbed his head, hoping that Sadie couldn't see how wide he was smiling. "He sounds like quite a character, but that's not surprising, I guess."

"Why's that?"

"Because he's related to you."

Isaac barely got the sentence out before Sadie mockingly chided him, "Oh, really?" She straightened fully, resting her hands on her hips.

After a few minutes of lighthearted repartee, things quieted down again. Without knowing what time it was, Isaac had no way of knowing just how long they had been walking, chasing lightning bugs and stargazing. Self-doubt stalked him like a barn cat hunting a field mouse. Was Sadie still having a good time? Would she want to head home soon?

Isaac pushed himself up and stretched to his full height. He brushed the grass from the seat of his trousers and sheepishly glanced around the darkness. "I suppose it's time to call it a night." He shrugged one shoulder. "Don't wanna get you home too late."

"Okay." Before he could extend his hand to help her, Sadie launched herself up from the ground. "Thank you for giving me a ride home."

Isaac assured her that it was his pleasure to see that she got home safely.

As they moseyed through the fields and back toward the few remaining courting buggies near the Beiler house, Sadie and Isaac walked in amiable silence. Occasionally they would pass by a drowsy mule that had chosen not to spend the night in the barn. Sadie stopped to soothingly pet each animal, wishing it a *gut* night. Isaac waited patiently for Sadie while she babied each creature, cherishing her gentle nature. Eventually, Sadie quickened her pace, and when she caught up with Isaac, he noticed her giggling softly.

"Did one of those mules tell you a joke?"

Sadie shook her head. "*Nee*, I was just thinking about how you were chasing lightning bugs with me. I've never seen you gallop like that." A few moments passed before Sadie spoke again, but this time her voice was filled with as much sweetness as one of Mim's strawberry pies. "I've never seen you smile so much either."

"*Jah*, well, chalk it up to the *wunderbar* company that I've had tonight." Even in the darkness, Isaac could make out Sadie's smile as clear as day. "Speaking of good company, let's see if there's still light in the windows when we pass Mim's house. I'd love for you to stop in and have a quick visit with *Mamm*. If you can give her just a smidgen of what you've given me tonight, it'll do her a world of good."

Isaac felt Sadie reach for his hand. She made a small, happy sound before she gave her answer. "I can't think of anything else I'd rather do."

Chapter Thirteen

❧

"Would you mind waiting here in the kitchen, just for a minute?" Isaac's voice was low when he led Sadie through the squeaking screen door and into Mim's house. "I just wanna make sure *Mamm* is...you know..."

Sadie nodded, understanding that Isaac needed to ensure that his mother was well enough to receive a visitor. "Of course. Take your time."

Isaac thanked Sadie, then pointed toward the oak cabinets on the opposite wall. "If you rustle around in there, you'll probably find a snack. Mim constantly bakes treats for the *kinner* who visit her. Help yourself!" With that, he went into the next room.

Though she appreciated Isaac's offer, Sadie didn't feel right about rooting through Mim's cabinets. Instead, she padded across the room to a small plant that decorated Mim's tidy countertop. She wasn't surprised to see that the African violet was in great shape, with the exception of three dead leaves. Sadie gingerly pinched off the few crumbly leaves, being careful not to damage the rest of the plant.

"Sadie, aren't you off the clock? Didn't think I'd see you gardening tonight, especially in my kitchen!" Sadie turned to see Mim entering the room, her waist-length hair neatly braided and slung over her shoulder. Wearing a floor-length nightgown and a terry cloth white robe, Mim appeared to have been thoroughly settled in for the evening.

Sadie tossed the three dead leaves into a nearby waste bin. "Force of habit. Sorry to just drop in when you're fixing to call it a night!"

"You're always welcome here. And, who am I to put a stop to a good habit?" Mim took a seat at the table and then motioned for Sadie to sit next to her.

Once Sadie was seated, Mim offered to fix her coffee or tea, which Sadie politely declined. "I just wanted to say a quick hello to Ruth. Feels like a long time since I've seen her."

Mim's eyebrows rose. "Came all the way here, at this hour, just to say hello, huh?" Sadie started to respond but bit her tongue instead. Mim was clearly privy to the fact that her nephew had attended the gathering earlier that evening. Surely, she didn't think it strange for him to take a girl home afterward, especially since he and Sadie were a courting couple. Mim quickly changed the subject after her gentle teasing. "Ruth perked up after you started coming around here. I can tell she missed seeing you regularly."

Sadie grimaced at the thought of Ruth's emotional suffering, but what a joy it was to know that Ruth found such significant comfort in their friendship. As she pondered their unlikely kinship, an idea whirred around inside Sadie's mind. "Do you happen to have a spare canning jar that I could borrow?"

Mim's lips parted with a puzzled expression. "Sure I do. I've got some in my storage room." Mim stood and shuffled across the floor in her worn, plain slippers. "What do you need a jar for?"

"Just thought of a way I could surprise Ruth."

Mim shrugged and disappeared around the corner, muttering to herself that she might turn out to be just as surprised as Ruth. A short time later, she returned with an empty jar and a lid. Sadie thanked Mim, then sprinted out of the kitchen and into the darkness, though she was careful not to slam the screen door behind her. Once she reached Mim's lawn, she unscrewed the jar's lid and placed the items side by side in the grass. Then Sadie scampered beneath the nearest tree and stood perfectly still until a green glow gradually buzzed closer to her. She gently captured the firefly, hurried back to the jar, coaxed the critter inside and tightened the lid. She repeated this about a dozen times until she was satisfied with her hunt.

Sadie took her twinkling jar up the porch stairs, through the screen door and into the kitchen. Mim had returned to her seat at the table and was now joined by her sister and nephew. Ruth appeared bright-eyed and eager, and though she was also dressed for bed, she didn't look the least bit weary. Sadie also noticed that a broad smile decorated Isaac's handsome face. She mentally warned herself that he would never be her real beau, so it would do no good to fancy him. A lump formed in Sadie's throat and she wondered if it was too late to give herself that advice.

"*Ach*, there you are, Sadie!" Isaac stood from the table and hurried to her side. "I didn't want *Mamm* to think I was fibbing after I told her she had a special visitor."

"I'd never want to make you look bad." As soon as the words left her lips, Sadie wished she could pull them out of the air and shove them back down. She gauged the room to see the reactions that her statement had received. Mim pursed her lips and quickly hurried to the stove to retrieve her kettle. She seemed to be forcing back an amused grin. Ruth's expression hadn't changed. Perhaps she hadn't heard. Isaac also didn't seem fazed by her tender words. Instead, he appeared downright giddy in anticipation of her and Ruth's reunion.

Deciding that she was overreacting, Sadie ventured over to Ruth, who surprisingly stood to greet her. Judging by their expressions, Mim and Isaac must have also been pleasantly stunned to see Ruth rise without prompting. When Ruth extended her arms, Sadie placed the jar on the table and gladly accepted Ruth's embrace. "Hi, Ruth. Seems like it's been years since I've seen you!" Sadie held Ruth close until Ruth started to pull away, wanting to give her all of the support she could absorb. When the lengthy hug came to an end, Ruth cradled Sadie's face in the palms of her hands, admiring the girl as if she were her daughter. Though Ruth still didn't smile, her eyes seemed much brighter than Sadie remembered them being.

Sadie encouraged Ruth to sit down so they could chat for a while. Understanding that Ruth wouldn't verbally communicate with her, it was plain to see that she enjoyed the company of her young friend. Sadie talked about a new restaurant that opened recently, her twin brother's new horses and the coming change in seasons. When she mentioned the upcoming cooler, shorter days, Sadie remembered the jar of fireflies.

"*Ach*, that reminds me! These little guys are for you," Sadie declared, reaching for the jar. As she handed the container to Ruth, the two women marveled at the little creatures as they crawled around their enclosure. "We're nearly at the end of August, so these might be the last lightning bugs we see this year."

Ruth stared down at the jar, watching intently as the insects explored the container. She glanced at Sadie, then back at the fireflies, as if they were the most unique sight she'd ever beheld.

"Maybe these little ones can brighten up the dark for you," Sadie gently suggested. "See how they light up when the others around them are lit up too?" Ruth reached for Sadie's hand and gave it a gentle squeeze. "*Jah*, all anyone needs is a small, steady light to see in the darkness."

What happened next stirred everyone in the room. The corners of Ruth's lips twitched, and a sound came from her throat as if she was about to cry. Instead, a smile slowly spread across her mouth that illuminated her face and softened her features. The weak grin turned into a sincere, pretty smile that was filled with emotion. Her complexion warmed and she appeared considerably younger, as if she were a brand-new woman.

Sadie's heart felt so full that she feared it would burst.

She'd never seen Ruth come this far out of her shell, nor had she seen a smile decorate the dear woman's face. She controlled her reaction so as to not startle Ruth. Out of the corner of her eye, she spied Mim wiping a tear from her cheek. Isaac, next to his aunt, had his hand partially covering his mouth, shielding a grin of his own. They both stood back and whispered between themselves, apparently nervous that even the smallest sound would disturb the moment.

Sadie continued talking quietly to Ruth for several more minutes before Isaac cautiously stepped forward. "Well, it's getting late," he hesitantly interrupted, placing his strong hand atop his mother's shoulder. "I should get our Sadie home before midnight, *jah*?" Ruth still didn't utter a single word, but she didn't stop smiling, and that was worth a thousand words.

As she and Isaac made their way back to the buggy, Isaac's words played over and over in Sadie's mind. *Our Sadie?* Did Isaac think of her as his, or was it simply an expression of everyone's collective fondness for her? She sincerely hoped it was the former.

The next morning, Sadie stood at the kitchen sink, staring out the window, elbow-deep in soapy dishwater. After a big breakfast, she and her younger sister went about tidying up. As Susannah finished wiping the table, she chattered about the first few days of her final year at the local one-room schoolhouse. Sadie cherished talkative Susannah, but she found herself unable to focus on her sister's schoolgirl tales. Instead, Sadie's thoughts drifted to the heartwarming events of the previous night.

Ruth had smiled for the first time since she'd known her, Sadie thought as she plucked a dish from the water and swirled a dishcloth over it. The Lord seemed to be working out things for His children. She grinned at the memories as she scrubbed the dish but was taken aback when a speck of her old, familiar burden floated into her mind. Would the Lord work things out for her too?

"I'll dry the dishes so we can get them put away faster," Susannah chirped as she bounded up to the sink. She gawked at the empty dish rack, looked up at Sadie and wrinkled her nose. "You've been scrubbing so long, I figured you'd be just about finished."

Sadie chuckled at her sister's direct comment. "Well, many hands make light work. We'll get this done in no time." She lifted the clean dish out of the water, causing a wave of suds to slosh onto Susannah's apron. Susannah scowled, then suggested that they get to work.

Deciding that Susannah could stand to lighten up, Sadie scooped up a handful of suds and rubbed them on her sister's cheek. This caused Susannah to playfully slap Sadie's arm with her dishrag. The tomfoolery went on for a short time but was interrupted by the sound of the back door creaking open.

A male voice interrupted the feminine giggles. "Looks like a war has broken out."

Startled, the sisters spun around simultaneously. There stood Isaac in the kitchen doorway, seeking permission to enter. Sadie placed a hand over her racing heart, endeared by the sight of him and itching to know the reason for his unexpected visit. Maybe he was there to tell her about how Ruth was feeling after last night's visit. Or maybe he was there just to see her, though she made sure to keep her composure in front of her younger sister and her guest.

Susannah let out a playful scoff and planted her hands on her hips. "My *schwester* always seems to find fun in every chore, even if all that fun means she takes twice as long to get things done."

"And here I thought I was brightening your day! See if I ever do that again!" Sadie crossed her arms as if terribly annoyed, but winked to be sure Susannah understood that she wasn't truly upset.

"Maybe it's good that I barged in," Isaac said as he stepped farther into the Stolzfus kitchen. "Someone should break up this fight." After everyone had a good laugh, Isaac's smiling eyes came to rest on Sadie. "Can I talk to you privately for a few minutes?"

Without hesitation, Susannah promptly exited the room. Even before Susannah was out of earshot, Isaac assumed her post at the sink. "I can help with the dishes since I interrupted your chores."

Sadie's heart was warmed by Isaac's thoughtful gesture. "A visit from a friend is never an interruption." She insisted that the dishes could wait, but Isaac was determined to help. Together they worked through the pile of dirty cookware, utensils and plates, making small talk for several minutes. When she felt her curiosity couldn't stand it any longer, Sadie gently nudged Isaac with her elbow. "Everything all right?"

Isaac pulled a clean plate from the dish rack and

began to dry it thoroughly. "Everything's just *wunderbar*, Sadie, and it's all thanks to you." Before she could respond, Isaac continued, his voice wavering slightly as if overcome with emotion. "Last night my *mamm* smiled. She smiled for the first time since the accident that took Rebecca's life."

Sadie dropped the fork she was scrubbing and flung her arms around Isaac's neck, wrapping him up in a tight embrace. "That's *wunderbar* news!" She recalled the previous evening's hushed excitement when Ruth smiled, but she hadn't realized that it had been Ruth's first in years.

Isaac held on to Sadie's embrace for longer than she expected, but she was glad to hold him close to her heart for as long as he needed. When they parted, Isaac seemed to ignore the dampness on his shirt from Sadie's wet hands and forearms. "It's a downright marvel! Somehow you managed to change my outlook on the future and breathe new life into my *mamm*'s spirit." When he reached into the sink to retrieve some clean silverware, his hand grazed Sadie's, causing her heart to flutter.

Sadie was unsure of how to react to Isaac's praise. "I just gave her a jar of lightning bugs, but I'm glad that they cheered her up," she reasoned as she handed the last clean dish to Isaac.

Isaac shook his head as he dried the plate. "A jar of bugs is worth more than money can buy if it makes *Mamm* smile." He glanced down at Sadie, grinning at her with obvious fondness. "I'd like to take you to dinner sometime this week."

Lightheartedly snatching Isaac's dishcloth from him, Sadie dried her hands. "Sounds like a date."

Isaac turned and leaned against the counter, crossing his arms over his middle. "Sure seems that way. We are courting, after all, ain't so?"

"*Jah*, I guess we are." Sadie's heart pounded. Just where was their relationship going? She had agreed to a phony courtship to keep her parents from fixing her up with any random fellow in the county, but the way that Isaac affectionately gazed at her made her question just how phony it was. Was she reading too much into his invitation simply because she so desperately pined to find love?

After Isaac departed, Sadie dashed up the stairs to her bedroom, needing some privacy to sift through the strange mixture of emotions that swirled like a twister through her. Shutting the door behind her, she made a beeline to her hope chest and took a seat on the lid. Unlike her sister's chest, Sadie's chest was mostly empty. She'd never seen a need to fill it with items to use in a home of her own. But soon she would be going on a date with her beau, who was really just a friend.

The giddiness she'd initially felt when Isaac had suggested dinner was alarming. Her first reaction hadn't been one of a friend eager to break bread with another friend. No, her feelings were much more significant. Was her newly realized crush on Isaac developing into stronger feelings? Using her finger to trace small hearts on the lid of the chest, Sadie fought back the urge to cry. She firmly reminded herself that their upcoming dinner was nothing more than time spent with a thankful friend, even though her heart painfully longed for something more.

Chapter Fourteen

On the following Friday night, Isaac and Sadie sat at a small table for two in a local, busy diner, enjoying their date. Isaac couldn't remember the last time he had so thoroughly enjoyed a meal, but he knew that Sadie's excellent company was the main reason behind his satisfaction. Their discussion flowed effortlessly, as usual, and it was filled with genuine laughter. The pair were so engaged in conversation that it took them nearly two hours to eat their meals, and an additional half hour passed as they chatted and finished slices of apple-pear cobbler, served with a scoop of cinnamon ice cream.

Isaac stared down at his half-eaten dessert and leaned back in his chair. "Don't think I can ever remember when I've felt so full or had such a pleasant time," he declared, playfully wiggling his eyebrows to emphasize the second half of his statement.

Sadie giggled as she broke off a piece of cobbler with her fork. "Isn't it funny that we came here tonight?

This was the same place where we agreed to feign a courtship."

Isaac spooned some ice cream into his mouth. "*Jah*, it's almost like it was meant to be."

Sadie suddenly dropped her fork on her plate. The clanging sound overpowered the murmur of all the quiet conversations happening in the restaurant. "Meant to be?" Sadie questioned, her eyes widening.

Feeling like all stares were on their table, Isaac cleared his throat nervously. His heart began to pound in his ears, realizing that his previous statement held a lot of weight to it. "*Jah, jah*. I mean…us agreeing to court solved both of our problems, so it's like the plan was meant to be."

Sadie stared at Isaac for several painfully long seconds before she grinned and took the final bite of her cobbler. "*Jah*, you're right!"

As Isaac finished his dessert, a chill swept through him that hadn't been caused by the ice cream. With some quick thinking, he'd avoided another near misunderstanding, though he wondered if his statement had been a peek into his true feelings instead of a mere slip of the tongue.

Sadie felt like the summer zipped by in the blink of an eye. Isaac stole her away for a few hours of companionship once every few days, much to her excitement. They enjoyed eating dinner together at various restaurants in the area, browsing the local farmer's market and occasionally going to the bank of Mill Creek to do some fishing. All of their outings proved delightful, but Sadie most enjoyed her lunch breaks when working at the greenhouse, now that Isaac had made a habit of showing up to share the noon meal with her.

On one overcast afternoon, Sadie stepped out of the greenhouse and headed for the small picnic grove tucked discreetly behind the building. With her tin lunch pail in hand, Sadie quickly spotted Isaac.

Her beau was seated at the picnic table closest to a cluster of white birch trees. With a paper bag and thermos placed in front of him, he politely waited for Sadie's arrival before he began to eat. *He's so courteous*, Sadie thought with a grin. He would make a good husband someday if he ever allowed a girl to love him again. Wishing she hadn't entertained such thoughts, Sadie shook off the hint of disappointment that poked at her, knowing that she'd never become Mrs. Isaac Hostettler, or married at all, for that matter.

As she approached the table, Isaac turned and smiled at her, then began rummaging through his paper bag. Triumphantly, he pulled out a hefty slice of pie. He turned around and held the pie in Sadie's direction, not realizing that she now stood directly behind him. "Taste this," he demanded, nearly shoving the dessert in her face.

"*Oll recht*, but can I sit down first?" Sadie feigned annoyance, but her rapidly spreading grin betrayed her.

Isaac shook his head. "Nope, you have to try a bite now."

Sadie took a seat next to Isaac. She took the slice of pie from him and unwrapped it. Ignoring the fork Isaac offered her, she bit into the pie as if it was a piece of fruit. Isaac burst into laughter and clapped his hands, but Sadie ignored his amusement. "Wow, this is *appenditlich*!"

Isaac seemed thrilled by Sadie's reaction. "I know! Guess who made it?"

Sadie took another bite of the cinnamon-apple pie, wondering why her friend was so obviously proud of the pie. "You?"

Isaac chuckled. "The only thing I know how to do in the kitchen is eat the food that comes out of it." He paused for a short time, as if gearing up to a big announcement. "*Mamm* baked it! She hasn't baked since the accident!" His eyes twinkled with excitement, like his greatest wish had come true. "She's putting effort into things again. She's getting out of bed in the morning without someone pushing her to do so." Isaac reached into the paper bag and retrieved another slice of the pie. As he unwrapped it, his smile spread from ear to ear. "This was Rebecca's personal recipe that she shared with *Mamm*. It's awful nice to taste it again."

"I'm so glad! The Lord heard our prayers for her, *jah*?" Sadie scooched closer to Isaac and gave him a quick hug. When he didn't embrace her in return but continued munching on his pie, Sadie slid back to her original spot and continued their conversation. "Ruth's been doing so well lately. Was she all right during the storm yesterday?"

Isaac's mouth twitched at Sadie's mention of rain, but he didn't look as sullen as he used to when damp weather was mentioned. "*Mamm*'s doing a lot better, but she cried for a while when it started to thunder."

He glanced toward the sky as if to make sure the clouds above weren't about to let loose. "Rain is never easy."

"For both of you?"

Isaac seemed to consider Sadie's question as he pulled a sandwich out of the paper bag, which Sadie assumed had been prepared by Mim. He gently pulled the crusts off the bread, a surprisingly precious action that warmed Sadie's heart. Then he responded, "I used to hate the rain. I don't hate rainy days anymore, but doubt I'll ever learn to love them."

"I see" was the only reply Sadie could muster.

They ate lunch in silence for a few moments before Isaac spoke up again. "I thought it was gonna rain the night that we went for ice cream with Rhoda and Mose. Damp days can be too cold for ice cream."

Sadie took another bite of Ruth's pie and nodded. "I don't think Rhoda and Mose would have been chilly, though, not with the way my *bruder* looks at her."

Isaac smirked before taking a sip of apple cider from his thermos. "They do seem to fancy each other an awful lot."

"That's an understatement if I've ever heard one," Sadie chuckled. "We'll be having a wedding here before too long."

Isaac's eyes grew as large as dinner plates. "Surely, you're not talking about them getting married this wedding season."

"You never know. They may surprise us."

Isaac popped the last bite of his sandwich into his mouth, then wiped his hands on his trousers. "Well, if they do tie the knot this year, it would be awful fast. They've only been courting for what…about two months?"

Sadie shrugged at Isaac's logic, shaking off a birch leaf that landed on her shoulder. "*Jah*, but they've known each other since childhood." Feeling a sudden rush of bravery, Sadie ventured into dangerous territory. "But either way, I suppose you can't deny that special feeling once it strikes you."

Isaac studied Sadie intently, as if trying to solve a difficult jigsaw puzzle. "I thought you've never been courted, but you sound like you've experienced love before."

Sadie was unable to look him in the eye as she tested the waters. Gathering her courage, she turned to face Isaac. "I haven't, but I can learn."

Sadie and Isaac met each other's gaze. He seemed to take her in, chewing on his tongue and apparently pondering her romantic statement. She waited for him to respond, and her heart longed for him to proclaim that he had feelings for her. Oh, if only this caring, gentle, handsome man would see in her what she saw in him. But, much to her dismay, Isaac said nothing. Instead, he chugged down the last of his cider.

Finally, Isaac sighed. Pressing his palms against the table, he stood and began to pack his rubbish into the paper bag. "Well, I've got to get going. I'm doing some repairs on Mim's buggy and I told her I'd have them done by tonight."

"Okay," Sadie quietly replied, scolding herself for being so bold, and wondering if she'd scared her fake boyfriend away. She bid him farewell, immediately losing her appetite. She stared down at the half-eaten slice of pie, wishing she'd never hinted at her growing, serious interest in him.

The rest of Sadie's afternoon was plagued with regret. As she arranged a display of birdhouses, watered the mums and swept the floor, Sadie pouted over Isaac's sudden departure. She'd been foolish to say something so forward, she thought to herself. Their relationship wasn't real, so she needed to stop treating it like it was.

At the end of her workday, Sadie was stopped by the teenage *Englisch* cashier. "That dude you had lunch with bought something for you." Bending down behind the counter, Madison reappeared with a large pot of yellow mums.

"Isaac bought this for me?" Sadie asked, doubting that she heard her young coworker correctly.

Madison dramatically rolled her eyes, as if explaining things further was a major inconvenience. "Well, I don't know his name. That cute guy who stops by every day to visit you picked this out, paid for it and asked me to give it to you at the end of your shift." She smacked on her chewing gum and blew a large bubble. "I think he likes you."

As Sadie's fingers caressed the delicate yellow petals, she recalled mentioning to Isaac many weeks ago that her favorite color was yellow. How sweet it was for him to have bought her the most beautiful plant that the greenhouse had to offer. Maybe he did care for her as more than a friend?

Imagining where the best spot would be to display the cheerful flowers, a concern interrupted Sadie's sudden burst of excitement. Was she mistaking his kindnesses for interest? Feeling the onset of a headache, Sadie rubbed her temples and sighed. It was all starting to become too much for her; she was suddenly feeling as if she was in over her head.

On the following Saturday, Isaac, Sadie, Rhoda, Mose and a few more of their unmarried friends decided to get together at the local miniature golf course for one last hurrah before the busy start of the harvest season, which would soon be underway. After a round of lighthearted mini golf, the group headed inside to enjoy some ice cream at the concession stand.

As he waited in line to place their order, Isaac turned to ask Sadie what flavor she'd like. He was surprised to see that she was no longer at his side. He looked around, but wasn't able to locate Sadie's pretty face, which always stood out in a crowd.

"Hey," Isaac whispered as he leaned between Rhoda and Mose, who stood in line in front of him. "Do you know where Sadie went?"

Mose glanced around the room. "Thought she was with you. Maybe she's in the washroom."

Rhoda shook her head as her mouth formed a small, concerned frown. "I was just in the washroom and no one else was in there. Maybe she went outside?"

Isaac stepped out of line and up to the window, then squinted through the sunshine that spilled into the parlor. There was Sadie, scurrying toward a small gazebo, hunched over slightly as she walked against the strengthening breeze. "*Jah*, you're right. She's headed for the gazebo."

Rhoda's usually sweet expression soured further. "By herself? Do you think she seemed a bit down today?"

"*Jah*, I noticed that too," Mose agreed, his concern for his twin evident in his tone. "She's been kinda quiet for the past few days. Wonder what's bugging her?"

Filled with senses of both responsibility and guilt, Isaac declared that he would check on Sadie. *Could she be upset because of me?* Isaac fretted as he hurried out of the concession stand and headed for the gazebo.

Come to think of it, he had abruptly left one of their lunch dates and hadn't returned for another one since. Truth be told, Sadie's insightful comment about the sensation of love had startled him to his very core. Sadie certainly had an unparalleled way with words, but how could she brilliantly articulate something she'd never experienced? How could she know what Isaac had been feeling stirrings of deep in his heart?

Sadie's innocent yet dead-on remark had forced Isaac to confront his attraction to her. Never in his wildest dreams had he imagined that he'd start to develop true feelings for another woman, and yet here he was, nearly unable to speak when Sadie half-heartedly smiled up at him from her seat on the gazebo's bench.

"The wind sure is picking up," Isaac pointed out as he stepped into the gazebo, placing a hand on his hat to keep it from sailing away like a tumbleweed.

"*Jah*, sure is," Sadie replied quietly with a grin that looked more like a grimace.

Isaac leaned against the post that supported the tiny

hut's roof. "We all thought maybe you got blown away." When Sadie continued gazing at the golden soybean fields just beyond the parking lot, Isaac's anxiety intensified. It wasn't like her to be so quiet. "Are you gonna come in and have some ice cream with us?"

Sadie shook her head, keeping her stare focused on the fields that would be harvested within the coming weeks.

Isaac rubbed his hands together to release some tension before taking a seat next to his beautiful friend. Something Mim had recently said came to the front of his mind, and he decided to see if her idea would cheer Sadie up. "Mim mentioned that she thought your and Mose's birthday was coming up soon. Is that right?"

Sadie studied Isaac curiously as the wind whipped the ribbons of her head covering around her face. "*Jah*, our birthday is on September 16."

"*Mamm*'s is on September 12, and Mim thought it might be nice to have a joint get-together to celebrate the September birthdays," Isaac told Sadie before his hat blew off his head. He jumped up and sprinted to catch it before it flew out of the gazebo, which caused Sadie to giggle.

"*Jah*, I think that sounds like a nice plan. It was nice of Mim to think of me and Mose," Sadie replied with a small smile and a quick, uneasy glance at Isaac.

"Mim said she remembered your birthdays because you are the only set of twins in this church district, and hearing of your birth was news that she would never forget," Isaac stated as he returned to his seat beside her. He sensed that something was off in their communication, like humid summer air before a thunderstorm rolled in.

"Is everything all right between us?" Sadie asked as concern contorted her lovely face, as if she'd read his mind.

"*Ach*, of course everything is all right," Isaac responded as he placed his arm around Sadie's slight shoulders. "What makes you think something is wrong?"

"You suddenly left in the middle of one of our lunches, and you haven't been back to see me since. Was it something I said?"

Isaac appreciated her directness. "*Nee*, not at all, Sadie." He felt her tremble, perhaps from the cool wind or maybe out of anxiety. Isaac decided to continue cautiously explaining himself. "I'm really enjoying the time we spend together and the unique bond we have." He paused, feeling his heart beat several strong thumps. "I guess I just don't know what to do with myself because I never expected to have such a close connection with someone ever again." He glanced at her nervously, then turned to stare at the same soybean field that Sadie had been focused on earlier. "I'm just…scared."

Sadie moved closer to Isaac and leaned against him, as if she knew that the gesture would comfort both of them. "I understand and feel the same way. Good to know we're on the same page."

Isaac agreed and did his best to remain calm so Sadie wouldn't notice that her nearness affected him. The pair talked for a short time before Isaac suggested they rejoin the group.

As he and Sadie headed back to the concession stand

to join their friends, Isaac greatly doubted that they truly were on the same page. They had agreed to fake a courtship for a short time to get themselves out of situations that neither one of them had wanted to be in. Yet Isaac now knew that he would not be satisfied with only a pretend, short-lived courtship.

What if he had a real shot at courting Sadie? Without a proper courtship, it would be impossible to fully understand his feelings for her. How was he to know if his attraction to Sadie was just puppy love or something much more? The warm feeling in him might be just infatuation with Sadie's positive, unique outlook. Or maybe he was afraid to love someone again and the static energy that he felt was only fear of the unknown.

And what would Sadie's reaction be if he were to suddenly confess his interest in her? Would she think their entire friendship was a farce? Was it even possible for them to have a real relationship now that things were becoming so complicated?

Isaac had so many questions, and so few answers…

Chapter Fifteen

"What did your *schwester* have to say in her letter?" Mim asked Isaac as she carefully frosted the large chocolate cake that she had baked the night before.

Isaac sat at the kitchen table, reading the note that had arrived in the mail from Judith, one of his five sisters. He glanced over the top of the page before scanning the letter once more. "Judith says that everyone back home is doing well. Our youngest sister, Rachel, just started eighth grade, and she's excited to graduate come next summer. Our eldest sister, Hannah, and her husband, Luke, are expecting a new *boppli* in April. Judith also mentioned that business has slowed down a bit in *Daed*'s woodworking shop. Without me being there to help, he got behind on several orders, so he's still keeping plenty busy." He placed the letter back in its envelope for safekeeping. "She also mentioned that everyone misses me and *Mamm*, and that I should tell you that everyone back home says hello."

"How nice," Mim replied as she spread the chocolate icing on the cake with a spatula. "When the mail came in, I saw several cards for your *mamm* postmarked from Indiana. It's nice that her *mann* and *kinner* want to celebrate her birthday even when she's not home with them." Mim glanced up from her icing and sighed. "Just look at the clouds! What a gloomy day for a party."

Isaac had also noticed the heavy gray clouds that had been rolling in throughout the morning but had chosen to ignore them. Today was a special day to celebrate his mother, Sadie and Mose, and he wouldn't let the threat of wet weather ruin the day. "We'll still enjoy ourselves even though we decided to move the party indoors," he stated confidently, though he knew that getting his mother outdoors would have certainly been preferable.

"*Jah*, and your *mamm* will have those nice cards and notes to read to distract herself from the weather," Mim declared, as if she had just read Isaac's mind.

Before he could respond, Isaac noticed some movement outdoors. There came Sadie, bounding up the porch steps, wearing a navy blue dress and an excited grin. "I think a little sunshine might be coming toward us after all," Isaac stated, knowing that Sadie's vibrant personality would brighten up even the gloomiest day.

Sadie stepped through the screen door and cheerfully greeted them. "Where's the birthday girl?" she asked as she took off her shoes and placed them neatly beside the door.

"Well, one just walked in the door," Isaac answered, causing both Sadie and Mim to chuckle. "The other one is taking a nap before the rest of our guests arrive."

Mim looked up from her work and glanced at the

small, plain clock that hung on the wall. "Speaking of guests, I thought I said that the birthday party would be starting at three o'clock. It's only noon."

Sadie shrugged as she moved to the counter, where Mim finished icing the cake. "I came to lend a hand with setting things up."

"Such a sweet *maedel* you are, Sadie," Mim gushed, giving Sadie a few pats on the shoulder. "Isaac already set up the extra chairs and put out some snacks while I was decorating the cake, so I'm afraid there's not much else left to do."

Though he was sure Sadie wasn't aware of it, her early arrival had given Isaac the perfect opportunity to present her with his birthday gift. It was something quite personal, and he felt that his particular gift would best be given away from curious onlookers. Leaving the letter from his sister on the table, Isaac stood and headed toward the door. "Would you like to go for a walk, Sadie?"

"*Jah*, that sounds nice!" She hurried over to her shoes and slipped them back on, as eager as a fish on land to return to water.

"Take umbrellas with you," Mim called to Isaac right before he stepped onto the porch. "Looks like the sky is going to let loose any minute!"

After he found two plain, black umbrellas in Mim's coat closet, Isaac and Sadie were on their way. Just as Mim had predicted, raindrops began to fall from the gray sky just a few minutes later. As he and Sadie made their way through Mim's barnyard, then into her overgrown fields, Isaac found himself not minding the rain for the first time in years. His lively conversation with

Sadie chased away any memories of the painful past, so much so that he barely noticed when the rain shower started to intensify.

"I'm glad Mim had the idea to celebrate all the September birthdays," Sadie said, breaking into Isaac's musings. "The Lord thought that each one of us was needed here on earth, so everyone must take time to celebrate the day they were born." She moved her umbrella to one side so she could see Isaac, seemingly unfazed by the mist that now lapped against her face. "What was your favorite birthday memory?"

"I'd have to say it was the year I turned twelve," Isaac shared. "My birthday is in December, and there had been decent snowfall that day. After *Mamm* cooked up an *appenditlich* birthday supper with all my favorite foods, *Grossdaddi* called all of us *kinner* outside. He'd hitched his old sleigh to one of the draft horses, who was wearing a harness full of bells. By the time we'd all clambered into it, *Grossmammi* came outside with thermoses of hot chocolate for us to pass around. *Grossdaddi* must've driven us around their farm for over an hour while we sang songs and sipped our cocoa. We probably would've stayed out longer if *Mamm* hadn't called us all back indoors." Isaac chuckled at the fond memory. "What was your best birthday?"

"This one is, of course," Sadie answered like she was surprised Isaac didn't already know the answer.

Isaac smirked at Sadie's response, wanting to hear more. "Why's that?"

"Well, because you're here. Having you and your *mamm* here in Lancaster County is the best gift anyone could ever ask for," Sadie stated as they approached a small grove of maple trees in the midst of one of the overgrown fields. "You're the best friend I've ever had."

As the pair ducked beneath the trees to get out of the rain, Isaac turned back and looked toward the barn. He suddenly realized that they had walked at least a half mile through soggy meadows. What would have normally felt like an endless, boring trek through uncomfortable, damp conditions had instead been filled with laughter and warm, meaningful conversations.

"I've got a little birthday present for you," Isaac announced, noticing his hands beginning to tremble when he set the umbrella on the ground. He reached into his pocket and felt around for the item he'd found for Sadie. Feeling his face flame with shame, Isaac stammered over his words. "To be honest, I'm…embarrassed. This is…well, it's such a tiny, dumb thing. I don't know if you could even call it a gift."

Sadie closed her umbrella and leaned it against the trunk of the nearest tree, allowing the canopy of leaves to shield her from the rain. She stepped forward curiously to see what Isaac had for her.

Isaac opened his hand, revealing a smooth, circular stone that rested in his palm. "I found this in Mill Creek one day while we were fishing." He handed the stone to Sadie, who readily accepted it. "I thought it was really something else. See, it's a perfect circle. And it's completely smooth from the water rushing over it for centuries." Isaac sheepishly rubbed the back of his neck, wishing he had something of greater value for Sadie, especially after all she'd done for him and his mother.

"It was just so unique, so I plucked it out of the creek and saved it for you. I knew if anyone would appreciate it, it would be you."

Sadie stared down at the flawlessly circular stone in her palm and said nothing for quite some time, causing Isaac's regret to flourish. He really should have gotten her something more substantial. Maybe a pair of binoculars she could use during her time spent bird-watching or perhaps a book about plants would have been better gift ideas. Too late now, he grumbled at himself, wishing with all his might that Sadie would see his good intentions.

Sadie finally looked up, causing a tear to roll down her cheek. "This is the most special gift I've ever received. I'll cherish this always." She closed her palm around the stone, then pressed it against her heart. "*Denki*, Isaac."

Relief swept through Isaac, and he now wondered why he'd doubted himself. Things always seemed to work out when it came to Sadie. "I'm glad you like it." He beamed, feeling heat still radiating from his face. "I knew you'd see the beauty in it."

"*Jah*," she replied in a near whisper that could barely be heard above the sound of raindrops pelting leaves. "Seems like we both did."

Isaac cleared his throat, taken aback by the sudden fluttering sensation in his chest. "We're always on the same page," he pointed out, the corners of his mouth twitching. Whenever Sadie was near, he couldn't seem to stop smiling. Just the thought of her spunky nature and pretty face was enough to trigger a grin that would last the whole day.

"*Jah*, we usually do think alike…except for now," she proclaimed with an impish grin. Using her free hand, she reached up, grabbed one of the tree branches above them and gave it a good shake, sending a torrent of water down on Isaac.

Isaac gasped and tried to step out of the way of the deluge. He hadn't expected a lighthearted prank so shortly after their sentimental moment. Sadie cackled as Isaac shook off the water that had collected on the top of his straw hat. Once Isaac placed the hat back on his head, he reached for another branch to shake some water on Sadie. Seeing what was coming, Sadie darted forward, attempting to run past Isaac and dodge his playful retaliation. As she dashed around him, she lost her footing on the wet ground and let out a shriek. Jumping into action, Isaac lurched forward, catching Sadie before she hit the ground.

Startled by the commotion and by the stirring deep in his heart, Isaac gazed down at Sadie, still cradled in his arms long after she had regained her balance. With their faces so close, Isaac's eyes searched Sadie's as he treasured this moment. Holding her safely in his arms felt completely natural, like she belonged close to his heart. As the rain continued to pour around them, Isaac's lips met Sadie's, and he felt like he was home. With his heart pounding in his ears, Isaac's instincts told him to pull away. But when Sadie rested her cool hands on both sides of his face, Isaac knew that he had been worried for nothing. A second sweet kiss followed the first, which felt like the warmth of summer sunshine.

When their lips parted, Sadie stood on the tips of her

toes, gently pressing her forehead against Isaac's, her eyes fluttering shut.

The monsoon-like conditions went unnoticed by the pair, still wrapped in an embrace. Stunned by the unexpected events of the day, Isaac continued to hold Sadie close. A part of him desperately scrambled to understand what this unexpected affectionate moment meant for their relationship. Another part of him never wanted their embrace to end.

As if she'd been struck by a sudden epiphany, Sadie gasped and stepped back. Her eyes snapped open and promptly glistened with tears. "I'm...I'm so sorry," she nervously sputtered. As if her heart had been freshly broken, her lower lip trembled like she was thoroughly riddled with sorrow. She spun around, hiked up the hem of her dress and bolted into the rain, charging through the drenched meadows like a startled mare.

Bewildered by Sadie's abrupt departure, Isaac stood motionless, alone beneath the cluster of trees. In one moment, their souls had lined up perfectly, and in the next, Sadie had run away as if her life depended on it. Had he done something wrong? Isaac started forward but stopped himself before chasing after Sadie. How could he comfort her without knowing what had upset her?

"Sadie!" He called for her several times before accepting that she wasn't coming back. *This is what I get for thinking I might find love again*, Isaac scolded himself, watching as Sadie's silhouette grew smaller and smaller in the misty distance.

Chapter Sixteen

❧

"Care for another slice of cake?" Mim asked Sadie after giving Ruth a second helping.

"*Nee, denki,*" Sadie quietly declined, doing her best to hide her searing heartbreak. She was pleased to see Ruth looking so well. Isaac's mother had come a long way since Sadie had first met her, but that wasn't enough to lift her spirits. She had barely been able to choke down one of the sandwiches her mother had brought to the party, let alone a second slice of cake.

"You sure, sis? Mim's cake is legendary, and we're celebrating our birthdays after all," Mose prodded from across the table. He forked a hunk of chocolate cake into his mouth before wiggling his eyebrows at her.

Sadie nodded and tuned out the lively conversation that was happening around the table. Mose, *Daed* and Susannah chatted about Mose's newest horse while Mim and *Mamm* talked about some of the articles they'd recently read in *The Budget*. Ruth eagerly listened as she ate her cake. Sadie stole a glance at Isaac and flinched when she saw him staring at her. He shot her a concerned, pleading look before she turned away, excusing herself to the washroom, lest she suddenly begin to weep in front of everyone.

As she left the table and hurried down the hallway, Sadie pressed her hand against her mouth to muffle the sobs that ached to be released. She entered the bathroom and shut the door just as the dam that held back her tears crumbled away. She pressed her back against the door, then slid to the floor in anguish. Letting her head fall into her hands, she wept as she recalled the events of the afternoon.

After her unexpected kiss with Isaac, Sadie had found time to run home, change into clean, dry clothes, and have a good cry in the privacy of her bedroom before it was time for her family to pile into their buggy and set off toward Mim's house. Since it was still raining cats and dogs, Mose couldn't take his open courting buggy, which meant the family of five had to crowd into the boxy, gray rig. It was a tight squeeze, especially in the back seat where Mose, Sadie and Susannah had to sit together, packed in like sardines, but Sadie didn't care. She had far too much weighing on her mind and heart to fret over an uncomfortable seating arrangement.

As the horse and buggy had rumbled down the quiet country lane, Sadie had tuned out the chatter of her family and the splashing of the buggy's wheels through the puddles. Instead, her mind had replayed the sweet kiss she'd shared with Isaac on what seemed like a never-ending loop, and each time she pictured the moment, another piece of her heart disintegrated into dust. She knew now, without a doubt, that she was in love with Isaac, much to her chagrin. She had agreed to court the man to avoid her parents' matchmaking and the pity-filled stares of her community, and she'd been foolish enough to have fallen in love. She was downright embarrassed, knowing that she'd given her heart to someone who only saw her as a friend. Surely, Isaac had only been caught up in the quiet, intimate moment under the shelter of the maple trees. More than likely, his kiss was nothing more than an impulsive mistake. Yet here Sadie was, in love with a man who would never be hers, and that hurt more than any physical pain she had ever endured.

"Hurry up, Sadie! Mim says it's time for gifts!"

Susannah's excited voice and her rapid knocking on the door brought Sadie back to the present. "I'll be right there," she responded as she scrambled to her feet. Thankful that her church district allowed for indoor plumbing, Sadie ran some cool water and splashed it against her face in an attempt to hide the evidence that she'd been crying. After patting her face dry with her apron, she took a deep breath before rejoining the festivities.

When Sadie entered the sitting room, she took a seat next to Susannah on the floor since all of the other seats were occupied. Mose had just been given high-quality work gloves from their parents, and he was now tearing the newspaper wrapping off a shiny new pocketknife from Isaac. Then Susannah presented Mose with the gift that she and Sadie had both chipped in on; a battery-powered lantern, which was something he'd mentioned wanting not too long ago.

Next, it was Sadie's turn. "Happy birthday, *dochder.*"

Anna smiled as she handed her eldest girl a gift. "This is from your *daed* and me."

Though Sadie was in no mood to celebrate her twenty-second birthday, she gratefully accepted the gift from her parents. She tore away the pink tissue paper to unveil a lovely leather journal. She flipped through the pages and noticed that a different scripture verse was printed on each page. She thanked her parents for the thoughtful gift before Susannah handed her a paper bag. Sadie peered inside and pulled out a battery-operated bird clock. A different bird's song would play each hour, on the hour. Susannah proudly stated that this gift was from her and Mose. Sadie thanked her siblings warmly. Finally, Mim handed Sadie a small basket filled with various floral-scented soaps. Sadie expressed her appreciation for the scented gift.

Finally, it was Ruth's turn for gifts. After Mim presented her sister with a pretty stationery set and Isaac gave his mother an ivy plant that he'd recently purchased at the greenhouse, Sadie stood and hurried into the kitchen, where she'd left the cloth bag containing Ruth's gift. When she returned to Mim's sitting room, she avoided Isaac's tense stare. Though her heart was broken beyond repair, she was determined to put on a pleasant smile. Sadie knew she would have to break off her pretend courtship with Isaac now that she had fallen in love with him, and this might be her last time spending time with his mother. She was determined to make this interaction with the dear woman a cheerful one, for Ruth's sake.

Sadie sent up a quick prayer for emotional strength

and knelt on the floor next to Ruth's rocking chair. "I made this for you," she explained, unfolding the colorful blanket. "It's a lap quilt."

Ruth draped the small quilt across her knees and ran her hands over the hearts and flowers Sadie had stitched into the fabric.

Sadie had to admit that the lap quilt looked quite different than any Amish quilt she'd ever seen. The pattern of hearts and flowers was almost chaotic. Because she found no pleasure in quilting, she didn't have as much experience as other Amish women her age. The stitches she made were noticeably uneven, though she had done the best she could when sewing it.

Ignoring her self-doubt, Sadie quietly pointed out features of the quilt to Ruth, explaining the thought behind each detail. "The flowers are to remind you of the ones we planted earlier this year, and the hearts are to remind you of how loved you are. I noticed you wear a lot of blue dresses, so I used as many shades of blue fabric as I could find."

Ruth's eyes shone with tears as her fingers traced one of the hearts on the blanket. She glanced at Sadie as her lips formed a trembling smile. She let out a little gasp, then stood and pulled Sadie into a warm, motherly embrace.

Sadie felt her own eyes filling with tears for what felt like the hundredth time that day. She not only loved Isaac, but she loved Ruth as well. Though Ruth had never uttered a single word to her, she felt like a second mother to Sadie. They understood each other without words, and Sadie knew in her heart that Ruth loved her. She was certain that this would make distancing herself from Isaac even more impossible than it already felt, but it was something that had to be done.

"Who's up for a game of Scrabble," Mim suggested, ending the bittersweet moment.

"I'll play," exclaimed Susannah as she collected all of the discarded wrapping paper. Ruth smiled and nodded in agreement, and Anna also stated that she thought a board game sounded like fun.

Amos stood and patted his stomach several times. "Think I'll have another slice of that cake."

"*Jah*, me too," Mose added, following his father into the kitchen.

"You both already had two slices," Anna protested in exasperation.

"We're celebrating, ain't so? I never heard of a celebration where folks limit themselves on sweets," Amos retorted, causing a round of chuckles from most of those in the room.

As they all filed back into the kitchen, Sadie felt someone tap her shoulder. Knowing it was Isaac, she didn't turn to face him. She knew she wouldn't be able to look him in the eye without falling to pieces, so she pretended to not have felt his touch.

"Can we talk, Sadie?" Isaac asked, his voice lowered so that only she could hear it. He reached for her again. This time he took hold of her hand, forcing Sadie to acknowledge him.

In her opinion, there was no need to discuss what had happened earlier that day. She loved him, and now Isaac knew it. Since he didn't love her in return, there was no use in hashing through things. "What's there to talk about?"

Isaac's eyebrows climbed high on his forehead and disappeared under his bangs. "I think you know."

Sadie glanced toward the kitchen table where a game of Scrabble was beginning between the women and where her father and brother were eating their third slices of cake. This was not the time to have a personal discussion, or for her to succumb to yet another puddle of tears. Giving her hand a strong shake to free herself from Isaac's touch, she shot him a pained glare. "Please, not here."

Isaac's mouth opened but before he could say something more, Sadie rushed away and joined the game of Scrabble.

The talk around the table remained just as lively as it had been earlier, though Sadie didn't contribute much to the conversation. Her heart felt so heavy that she felt like she couldn't breathe and had trouble paying attention to the game. Whenever it was her turn to play a word, she either played the most simple word she could, or opted to pass to the next player. She glanced up from her letters and noticed Isaac sitting with her father and Mose. Instead of joining in their conversation, he stole several sad glances at Sadie, like he was an abandoned puppy dog.

As evening approached, the Stolzfus family began to say their goodbyes and thank Mim, Ruth and Isaac for the nice afternoon they had shared. After a quick farewell to Mim and Ruth, Sadie slipped out of the house, hopefully unnoticed. Carrying her birthday gifts, she dashed through the rain and into Mim's barn, where her family's horse happily munched on oats in one of the empty stalls. Soon her father would come out to the barn and hitch the horse to the buggy, and her family would be on their way home. Then she would get ready for bed and do her best to forget this, the most sorrowful day of her life.

Isaac couldn't believe it when Sadie quietly exited the house as her family lingered, having some final conversations with Mim. He felt as if he'd been slapped across the face by the way she'd acted toward him this afternoon. Didn't Sadie have anything to say about the kiss they'd shared under the trees, or her emotional exit afterward? Why had the tender moment upset her so much? How were they to go about their lives when such a delicate problem had wedged its way between them?

Deciding that he couldn't let her leave without clearing the air, Isaac excused himself from the kitchen, shoved his feet into his boots and rushed out to the barn. Running between the raindrops, he did his best not to slide through the mud in the barnyard. Sadie's *daed* had tucked their carriage into the barn to keep it out of the rain, so he was sure Sadie would be nearby. When he entered the barn, he felt his heart stop for a moment when he laid eyes on Sadie as she stroked the face of her family's horse, looking downright miserable. He'd never seen such a dejected look on her lovely face, and quite frankly, it scared him to his core.

"Sadie," Isaac called, nearly tripping over his untied bootlaces. "We need to talk."

Seeing him, she quickly climbed into the boxy buggy and planted herself in the back seat.

Bounding up to her rig, Isaac grabbed one of the

buggy's wheels to keep it from carrying Sadie away, even though there was no horse hitched to the rig. The pair stared at each other, neither one of them saying anything for a time. It was dim in the barn, but there was enough gray light spilling in from the wide-open doors to allow him to see something unfamiliar in Sadie's eyes. Unease. Despair.

"That was a real nice lap quilt you gave *Mamm* for her birthday," he started, trying to break the ice between them. "I was surprised since I thought you didn't like to quilt."

"I don't," Sadie replied glumly as she fiddled with the hem of her dress apron, yanking on a thread that had come loose.

"Why'd you sew a little quilt, then?"

"Because I love her. Love changes people."

Once again, Sadie's direct answer floored Isaac. Rather than continuing their small talk, he decided to get to the point. "I'm sorry about…what happened earlier."

Sadie hung her head for a moment. "Don't be sorry." Picking her head up, she gazed at Isaac with the most feeble smile he had ever seen. "I guess for a moment we both thought our courtship was real," she whispered as tears began to well up in her eyes.

Taken aback by Sadie's explanation of their kiss, Isaac let go of the buggy wheel. She'd hit the proverbial nail on the head. Oh, his heart nearly shattered at the sight of her looking so sullen. He longed to climb into the buggy, gather her into his arms and soothe whatever was making her so sorrowful. Wondering if embracing her would do more harm than good, Isaac heaved a sigh, unsure of what to say or do. "*Ach*, Sadie."

Sadie wiped her eyes on the sleeve of her dress, then cleared her throat. "Ready to go?" she asked in a much lighter tone. Isaac turned to see who she was talking to and was disappointed to see the rest of the Stolzfus family running into the barn to get out of the rain.

"*Jah*, we'll just hitch up Samson and be on our way," Mose called back to his twin. He and Amos made quick work of readying the horse to leave while Susannah and Anna joined Sadie in the buggy.

The sudden arrival of Sadie's family forced an end to the conversation that Isaac was having with Sadie. Whatever had gone wrong between them was still unresolved, and Isaac hated to let Sadie leave on a bad note. But with her family there to hear every word they would say, what else could he do? He helped Mose and Amos prepare their horse, then followed the buggy out of the barn as it departed.

For the second time that day, Isaac watched Sadie leave as he stood alone in the rain. While the horse and buggy clip-clopped down the drive, then out to the lane, Isaac felt sick with anxiety. What in the world had upset Sadie so much? Did she regret their kiss? Dragging his hands down the sides of his face, Isaac felt like a piece of him had died, and he wondered if he'd lost his dearest friend.

Isaac hauled himself back into Mim's house, then without saying a word to his mother or aunt, he went upstairs to his dark bedroom. Without even taking off his wet boots, Isaac collapsed against the mattress. He stared up at the ceiling, emotionally drained and too exhausted to fret anymore.

Some time later, Isaac turned when his door creaked open ever so slightly. Mim and her gas lantern peeked into his room with the silence of a church mouse. As if she'd expected him to be asleep, Mim let out a little gasp when she saw her nephew stir. "Sorry, just making sure you're *oll recht*. We didn't see you after Sadie and her family went home."

"I'm fine," Isaac fibbed to not worry his dear aunt. "Just tuckered out." He noticed Mim was wearing her nightgown and robe and her hair was in its usual bedtime braid. Several hours must have passed since he'd come upstairs.

"Hmm," Mim responded, sizing up Isaac as if she didn't quite believe him. She noiselessly stepped into the room and took a seat in the rocking chair near the window. "Sadie's an awful nice girl, *jah*?"

Isaac bit his tongue. Had Mim come to pry? Frankly, he was far too exhausted to discuss Sadie's positive attributes. "*Jah*, she sure is." Sitting up, he slid to the foot of the bed in order to better see his aunt. Might as well get this conversation over with.

Mim paused before speaking again, seemingly to choose her words carefully. "Before Sadie started paying visits around here, your *mamm* barely functioned. Do you remember how she'd lay in bed all day, not even getting up to eat?"

"*Jah*, of course," Isaac replied solemnly, wondering why Mim had chosen to bring up such a grim topic.

"Through her actions, Sadie showed the love of the Lord to your *mamm*. It took some time, but when she allowed Sadie to love her, she started coming out of her shell."

Still uncertain of the purpose for Mim's midnight visit, Isaac voiced a question that he'd asked himself every day for the past two years. "Do you think *Mamm* will ever speak again?"

Mim smiled lovingly at her nephew, her wrinkles appearing deeper in the glow of the lantern. "I don't know, Isaac. We can pray for that." She stood and shuffled across the room, hesitating by the door. "Sometimes a person just needs to let themself love another person. The harder you fight love, the more difficult you'll make your life." Mim shrugged, as if her vague advice could be taken or left, then walked out of the room. *"Gut nacht,"* she said silently, closing the door behind her.

Still seated on the edge of his bed, Isaac's sight readjusted to the darkness now that Mim and her lantern had left. With his elbows planted on his knees, he cradled his head in his hands. Mim was absolutely correct. He'd unknowingly complicated the future when he'd invited Sadie into a false relationship. Life had been difficult since he began repressing his feelings for her. The courtship of convenience had turned into a major inconvenience, now that serious emotions were involved.

How would he ever smooth things over with Sadie? Was there any hope for them as a real couple? Dozens of questions swirled in Isaac's mind, but there was one thing he was certain of.

He loved Sadie Stolzfus with all of his heart.

Chapter Seventeen

On the following Tuesday afternoon, after the scholars had left the little one-room schoolhouse, Sadie and Rhoda entered the classroom armed with cleaning supplies. Rhoda would be filling in as the substitute teacher for the next two weeks while the usual teacher, her sister, Sarah Mae, recovered from a sprained ankle.

Rhoda had decided to clean the schoolhouse from top to bottom as a gesture of kindness, and she had politely enlisted Sadie as an assistant. Always eager to lend a hand to anyone who asked for help, and even those who didn't, Sadie had readily accepted the invitation. The chore of tidying the schoolhouse that she had attended years ago would hopefully bring on cheerful, nostalgic memories. Thoughts of a happier time might allow her to escape from the constant gloom that had plagued her over the past few days, all of which had felt dismally endless.

First, Rhoda washed the windows while Sadie polished each one of the wooden desks. Then they moved on to washing the chalkboard and filling the gas lamps. After the shelves were dusted and every inch of the floor had been swept, Rhoda and Sadie gave the timeworn floorboards a good scrubbing. As they washed the floor, Rhoda talked about her sister's injury and the upcoming double date that she and Mose had planned with Leah Beiler and her beau, Daniel. Sadie, however, was feeling far less sociable. She did her best to keep up with Rhoda's chatter, but her mind continued to drift to painful thoughts of Isaac.

Since their unexpected kiss, not an hour had passed without an image of Isaac popping into her thoughts. She felt that she was at her breaking point, and had firmly decided that the only way to carry on with her life was without Isaac. The notion that she cared so deeply for him but would never truly be his was enough to make her nauseous. Unfortunately for Sadie, Isaac wasn't going to let go of their friendship without an explanation as to what had gone wrong between them. Yet Sadie couldn't bring herself to look Isaac in the eye, declare her love for him, then face certain rejection.

That past Sunday had been particularly difficult since Sadie had been forced to be near the man who lingered in her mind and haunted her dreams during the church gathering. Countless times she'd felt Isaac's cheerless gaze land on her, and she found it impossible to concentrate on the preaching. On that particularly stressful Lord's day, Mose had sheepishly approached Sadie before the church meal with a message from Isaac. "He just wants to know if you're all right."

Assuming that her twin brother knew nothing of their fractured relationship, Sadie had put on her bravest smile and replied with a single word. *"Jah."*

Tears rushed into Sadie's eyes as she recalled the events of the past week, and she scoured the schoolhouse floor with even more vigor. Was it wrong to simply disappear from Isaac's life without an explanation? As cruel and painful as it was for both of them, Sadie saw no other option. *Oh, Lord, help my aching heart to heal*, she prayed as tears fell from her cheeks and splashed into the sudsy water on the floor.

"We've got quite a lot done in here, so I think we deserve a break." Rhoda sat back on her heels as she wiped her brow with her wrist. "I brought some chocolate-mint whoopie pies for a snack. Would you care for one?" When Sadie didn't answer, Rhoda glanced at her friend, deep concern quickly spreading across her freckled face. "*Ach*, Sadie! *Was iss letz?*"

"I've...I've got to confess something to you, Rhoda," Sadie stammered, unable to stop her flow of tears. "It's just *baremlich!*"

Rising from her spot on the floor, Rhoda hurried over to Sadie and sat beside her. "What's terrible?" she asked, drying her hands on her black apron.

Sadie was on the verge of hyperventilation and it took several moments before she was able to speak. "What do you know of my friendship with Isaac?"

"*Ach*, I don't know!" As a blush spread like a wildfire across her entire face, Rhoda's brow creased, like she sensed something was amiss. "You two are a couple, ain't so?"

Sadie hung her head, her heartbreak intensifying when she saw that she had deceived her friend with her actions, despite the fact that she hadn't told a single lie. "Isaac and I have been courting, but only for show."

Rhoda tilted her head as if she didn't fully understand. Sadie choked on a sob and wiped away the tears that flowed down her flushed cheeks. "Earlier this summer, Nancy Beiler was on the hunt for a beau, and she set her eyes on Isaac. Do you remember?"

Rhoda chuckled quietly, which took Sadie by surprise. "*Jah*, of course I remember. She caused quite a scene over him on a few occasions."

Sadie took a deep breath and shuddered, unable to control her weeping. "Isaac was still recovering from the loss of the girl he'd planned to marry. When Nancy showed that she was interested in Isaac, he asked me to fake a courtship with him, just until Nancy lost interest and set her sights on someone else."

"But Nancy moved on to chasing Johnny Glick not too long ago. You're saying you kept this up for…what, nearly two months?" Rhoda asked.

Sadie winced as she was filled with regret and embarrassment. "*Jah*, we did."

Rhoda smiled sympathetically, brushing a tear away from Sadie's clammy cheek. "Why?"

"It hurts knowing I'll never get married or have a family of my own. It hurts knowing that I don't belong anywhere, and everyone else knows it too. My parents threatened to play matchmaker and fix me up with someone in our church district." Sadie hiccupped, feeling like a wagon wheel that was stuck in a deep mud puddle. She exhaled with exasperation, feeling like she had no tears left to cry. "I'm so ashamed of myself. I wish I'd never agreed to court Isaac just for show."

"I'm sorry you're hurting so much. Sounds like you

were only trying to help a friend who was in a sticky situation, while also being stuck in one of your own," Rhoda whispered, inching closer to her tearful companion. She embraced Sadie, stroking her back and allowing her to cry. "I just wish you knew that you were never truly alone."

Though she was not comforted by Rhoda's kind words, Sadie appreciated her friend's devout support and understanding. "*Denki*, Rhoda."

The two young women continued sitting on the floor while Rhoda patiently allowed Sadie plenty of time to compose herself before she spoke again. "Can I be very frank with you, Sadie?"

"Of course!"

Rhoda's fair, rosy cheeks flamed an almost auburn color, which let Sadie know that she was about to say something that might be difficult to hear. "Isaac is a good man, and I don't think he intended to hurt you. But, in his pain, I don't think he realized that asking you to be his fake *aldi* isn't at all fair to you." She paused, apparently gauging Sadie's reaction. "It also wasn't fair for you to court him just to keep folks from pitying you."

Truth be told, Rhoda wasn't wrong. None of this was fair to either of them, though spending so much time with Isaac for appearance's sake had never felt like a chore to Sadie. In fact, those months had been the most joyful time in her life. A small spark reignited deep in her soul and she felt the need to defend the phony courtship. "It wasn't all bad. We had a lot of fun and got to know each other real well."

Rhoda mulled over Sadie's argument. "But what if… what if there is some fellow out there who is genuinely interested in courting you? He wouldn't be able to do so because of this…arrangement…that you've got with Isaac."

Staring down at the nearly dry, spotless floor, Sadie shrugged and flung her scrubbing rag into the nearby bucket. "That'll never happen."

"Don't say that." Rhoda attempted to reason with her dejected friend. "You don't know if another man will strike your fancy someday!"

"It won't happen," Sadie protested confidently.

"Sadie…"

"It won't happen because…I…I love Isaac!" Saying aloud the private words that she'd kept hidden in the deepest corner of her heart summoned a fresh round of tears. "I can't imagine ever loving anyone else as much as I love him!"

"That's *wunderbar*," Rhoda exclaimed with a squeal. Her sudden cheer was certainly a stark contrast to Sadie's misery. "You're already practically a couple. You should be honest with him and tell him how you feel. Wouldn't that solve everything?"

"It's not that simple." Sadie moped as she accepted the handkerchief Rhoda handed her. Rhoda didn't know about their kiss, and how Isaac apologized for it. An apology meant he regretted that special moment with her. Sniffling like she had a severe cold, Sadie shook her head. "How am I supposed to tell him how I feel? We were supposed to be faking a relationship, not experiencing a real one!" Noticing a loose thread at the hem of her evergreen dress, she yanked on it hard, causing a small tear. "He'll think I'm pathetic, if not downright ridiculous."

Rhoda frowned, seeming to fully understand the weight of Sadie's emotional burden. "This can't go on forever, though. Won't you continue to suffer unless you confront this situation?"

"I don't know." Sadie rubbed her temples. "I'm at my wit's end." It only then dawned on her that she had more to worry about than simply avoiding Isaac until she figured things out. "What about Mose? If you thought Isaac and I were courting, he probably does too."

Rhoda fondly placed her hand on Sadie's shoulder. "Nothing to fret over. He's your *bruder*." Rhoda's mouth contorted like she was suppressing a wide grin. The thought of her beau probably tickled her pink, but she respectfully kept her excitement at bay. "If anyone would understand, it would be your twin. I never saw siblings who have a closer relationship than you two."

Staring down at the torn hem of her dress, Sadie heaved a weighty sigh. "We've always been so truthful with each other. He'll be disappointed in me."

"I don't think you need to worry, but how about I explain everything to Mose?"

Sadie nodded wistfully, truly grateful for Rhoda's sincere compassion. "*Denki*, Rhoda. You're the truest friend anyone could ever ask for."

Rhoda's silver eyes lit up at Sadie's compliment. "Friends pray for each other, *jah*? Let's pray right now that both you and Isaac will find peace."

They bowed their heads in silent prayer as they sat on the squeaky-clean schoolhouse floor. The gesture was severely needed, though something restless in Sadie doubted that prayer could help their struggles at this point.

Chapter Eighteen

The start of the harvest season was just beginning and Isaac noticed a farmer and a team of mules working in the fields at nearly every farm his buggy passed by. The earthy scent of the ground being woken from the calm summer growing season was a welcome comfort to Isaac's weary soul, and he was certain that his mother felt the same way. This short errand to the Mennonite-owned bulk foods store was her first trip out of Mim's house since they had arrived in Bird-in-Hand, besides church meetings, and she seemed to be thoroughly enjoying their noontime outing.

Mamm leaned out of the buggy ever so slightly and tilted her face upward, deeply inhaling the fresh air that was filled with little hints of the coming autumn. A smile crossed her lips as she closed her eyes when the sunshine warmed her face.

Sadie would do the same thing, Isaac was certain. Maybe that's why she and his mother felt drawn to each other. It was a bittersweet notion. This outing was a substantial positive step for his *mamm*, which normally would have thrilled Isaac, but how could he be truly content when things felt so bleak between him and Sadie?

It was only the last week of September, but the past ten or so days felt unseasonably chilly, though Isaac knew that it seemed bitter and endless due to the absence of Sadie's spiritual warmth. After he'd sent two letters and a vague message through Mose, then one through Rhoda, Sadie still remained unresponsive. Twice he had traveled to Sadie's house to demand to speak with her, and both times he'd turned his buggy around before it reached the Stolzfuses' driveway, fearing that he would only push her farther away with an unannounced visit. Regardless, things were coming to a boiling point and soon Sadie would have to hear him out, or else he would just have to accept that love just wasn't meant for him. He'd given his heart to two different women, and wouldn't give it away a third time.

As they entered the grocery shop, Isaac held the door open for his mother. The gentle hymns that played in a bluegrass style over the store's speakers offered a rare dash of peace, which Isaac's soul absorbed immediately. He decided that the mellow praise music was a sign from the Lord that he should take comfort. It was a sunny day and his mother had willingly accepted his invitation to leave the house. Though his heart longed for Sadie to the point that his chest ached, he was determined to be content, if only in this moment at the bulk foods store.

When he approached a small selection of local dairy

products, Isaac stopped in his tracks. There was Mose Stolzfus, staring grimly at the coolers filled with rows of local milk. Mose suddenly turned, probably hearing the squeaky wheel on Isaac's shopping cart, and his face brightened with a welcoming grin. *Oh, great. So much for not thinking about Sadie right now.*

"Isaac! Ruth! How are you?" Mose's eyes grew as large as the watermelons in the nearby produce section when he saw Isaac's mother, but he graciously didn't mention the surprise he was certainly feeling.

"We're doing *gut*," Isaac fibbed for the sake of his mother. "Figured we'd run some errands for Mim since we're finally having a sunny day after that rainy spell."

"Jah." Mose bobbed his head. "When I get back to the house, I'm fixing to help my *daed* harvest our north tobacco field."

Isaac rubbed his chin. "Sounds like a good idea. Maybe I'll help Mim in her vegetable patch when we get home. It's a shame that she has about sixty acres of empty pasture just going to waste." He shrugged. "I tried convincing her to let me farm it for her, but she thinks it's too much work for me to do alone. She's getting up in years and can't pitch in with that sort of labor."

Mose nodded understandingly. "Well, maybe in the future she'll change her mind. Where the Lord leads, He always provides."

"Jah," Isaac agreed so quietly that he barely heard his own response. *"Mamm,"* he began while turning to his mother, "would you mind if Mose and I talked privately for a spell?" Ruth said nothing but smiled and nodded as she took the shopping cart from Isaac and

pushed it away. Once his mother was out of earshot, Isaac turned his attention back to Mose. "What's got you looking so worried?"

Mose scoffed and waved a hand through the air as if he wasn't truly bothered by anything. "Milk prices aren't so good right now." He gestured toward the cooler, pointing at the listed prices. "It's starting to worry me since I'll be partnering with my *daed*'s dairy operation next month." Mose shuffled his feet and peered around the corner as if to make sure that they were still alone. "Rhoda and I are getting hitched come the wedding season, so I wanna make sure I can provide for her. Please keep that under your hat, though."

Isaac did his best to muster a genuine smile for his friend. Indeed, he was truly happy that Mose and Rhoda had found love, though he couldn't swallow the hard lump of jealousy that formed in his throat. "That's *wunderbar*, Mose! Don't worry yourself too much about the future." Isaac recited Mose's earlier proverb with a reassuring grin. "Where the Lord leads, He always provides."

The two men stood silent and politely smiled as an *Englisch* customer passed by with two curious children. After the brood had moved on, Mose nodded toward Ruth, who was studying the wide selection of generic cereals at the other end of the long aisle. "It's real nice to see your *mamm* out and about. Don't think I've ever seen her outside of church, or looking so well, for that matter."

Isaac inhaled so quickly that it caused him to have a short coughing fit. His spell was brought on by thoughts of Sadie stampeding into his mind. He'd been able to focus on the small talk between himself and Mose, but now Sadie was at the front of his mind again, which derailed Isaac's ability to keep his emotions in check. He cleared his throat several times, doing his best to keep his tears at bay. They itched to be shed, but he refused to give in to his anguish, since doing so ran the risk of his mother noticing.

Mose immediately noticed Isaac's dramatic shift in mood. *"Was iss letz?"*

Isaac cleared his throat once more. "It's Sadie. It's her gentle, kind ways that nursed *Mamm*'s spirit back to health."

Mose smiled, though his grin seemed cautious. "That does sound like our Sadie."

Isaac pinched the bridge of his nose and closed his eyes. "It's not just my *mamm*'s progress, though. Sadie made everything better for her, and for me too." He opened his eyes. "She made everything whole, and I broke it."

"The fake courtship, *jah*?"

Unable to make eye contact with Mose, Isaac stared into the freezer, feeling as cold as the contents kept frozen inside it. "She told you about that, did she?"

Mose shook his head. "No, Rhoda filled me in on those details. I guess it was bothering Sadie so much that she spilled the beans to Rhoda. Sadie was so upset that she couldn't bring herself to tell me, so Rhoda shared the news." Mose rolled his eyes. "Silly, though. Sadie knows she can trust me with anything. I'm her twin."

Isaac shifted uncomfortably and he glanced over his shoulder to make sure his mother was still too far away to overhear their sensitive, quiet conversation. "I'm at a loss, Mose. Sadie won't respond to any of the letters I've sent. I also tried to reach out to her through both you and Rhoda." Exasperated, Isaac took a moment to catch his breath. "It's like…like the best thing that ever happened to me has gone missing, and I'll never find it again!"

One corner of Mose's mouth turned upward. "Sounds like your fake courtship was more real than you expected."

Isaac let out a pent-up sigh. "*Jah*, I love Sadie. More than anyone or anything else."

Mose's crooked smile straightened into a full-on grin, though it quickly faded into a much more serious expression. "Can I give you some advice?"

"Sure," Isaac replied, eager to hear words of wisdom from someone who had known Sadie for his entire life.

"Collect your thoughts. Pay Sadie a visit, and be honest with her. Tell her how you feel, before you lose her forever."

Isaac thanked Mose for his advice, though he wondered if it had been given just a little too late.

"Sure thought Ruth and Isaac would be back by now," Mim commented to Sadie as they sat in side-by-side rocking chairs on her front porch. "I thought they were only going to Bird-in-Hand Bulk Foods, but knowing Isaac, he probably stopped to treat Ruth to lunch. She's been doing so much better lately, so it wouldn't surprise me if he's trying to get her out of the house for as long as possible."

Sadie took a sip of the meadow tea Mim had given her, gripping the glass with a trembling hand. As much as she enjoyed socializing with Mim, that wasn't the purpose of her visit. She was there to officially break off her feigned courtship with Isaac, and prolonging this dreaded visit was making her antsy. When she'd arrived several hours ago and Mim had told her that Isaac wasn't there, Sadie'd had half a mind to turn and head for home. Knowing that she would only have to work up the courage to face the uncomfortable conversation once again, she'd decided to stay and try to enjoy Mim's company until Isaac returned.

"I'm awful glad to hear that Ruth's feeling so much better," Sadie finally replied after finishing her drink. "She looked like she was doing real well at the last church services. Maybe soon she'll start to speak again."

"We can pray for that." Mim let out a contented sigh. "The Lord still works miracles, *jah*?" Sadie didn't comment on Mim's expression but nodded in agreement. A few silent seconds passed while Mim glanced at Sadie's empty glass. "Can I get you more to drink?"

Sadie shook her head, fearing that her nervous stomach wouldn't settle if she had another glass of tea. *"Nee, denki."*

"Just holler if you change your mind." Mim slowly stood with a grunt and made her way toward the screen door. "The Lapp *kinner* usually stop by for a visit after school and I don't have any sweets to give them, so I better start baking. Wouldn't want to disappoint those cute little faces," Mim said to herself more than to Sadie.

"Want me to lend a hand?" Sadie offered half-heartedly, not wanting to appear rude.

"No need," Mim declined. "Besides, you're here to see Isaac, and you'll want to know the minute that he arrives home. I can tell you've got something important to discuss." Sadie glanced up at Mim, her eyes sparkling with surprise, startled by her observation. "It will be *oll recht*," Mim declared as she gave Sadie a reassuring pat on the shoulder. "Talk to the Lord about it, not just my nephew." With that, she headed inside to start her baking.

Sadie glanced around the now empty porch, noticing as a breeze gently nudged one of the porch swings into a swaying motion. How she wished that Mim had remained outside with her until Isaac arrived. Now that she was alone, she had no distraction and was all the more jittery.

Alone. Alone on the porch and alone for the rest of her life. Unless Isaac suddenly made a declaration of love for her, Sadie would spend the rest of her days without a husband or a family of her own. The time had come to finally give up on her dream of sharing her life with someone whose heart sang the same song as hers. If she couldn't spend her life with Isaac, she wouldn't spend her life with any man.

Refusing to succumb to self-pity, Sadie took Mim's advice and decided to spend some time in prayer. As she closed her eyes and bowed her head, she thanked the Lord that He had finally given her the courage to confront the moment she had been avoiding, and for the strength to face each new day knowing that she would never find reciprocated love.

The clip-clopping of a horse's hooves and the rumble of buggy wheels caused Sadie's eyes to snap open. With her heart pounding so strongly that it echoed in her ears, Sadie lifted her head. She instantly recognized the horse as Shadow, with his unmistakable gray coloring. Isaac and Ruth had finally returned home from their outing.

"Lord, please guide my steps and guard what's left of my heart from breaking," Sadie whispered as she stood from the rocking chair. She took several deep breaths in an attempt to settle her nerves. The time had come. The joyful, satisfying, comfortable days that she spent with Isaac were about to come to an end. She started forward, taking the porch steps two at a time. One step closer to her future as an old maid. One step closer to being alone, she thought as tears formed in her eyes.

A ray of sunshine peeked around a passing cloud, warming Sadie's face as she plodded onto Mim's front lawn. At that moment, the heart-to-heart conversation that she and Rhoda had shared while cleaning the schoolhouse shot to the front of her mind. Sadie repeated Rhoda's sentiment aloud, suddenly seeing it in a new light. "I wish you knew that you are never truly alone."

At the time of their conversation, she'd assumed Rhoda had been referring to herself, and maybe Mose or the other members of her family. No, Rhoda had been referring to the Lord, Sadie realized with a bittersweet smile that stopped her flow of tears. With the company and love of her creator, she would never truly be alone. For the first time in weeks, Sadie felt an unfamiliar yet unmistakable sense of peace about her relationship with Isaac, and about her future, regardless of what might lie ahead.

Though she was only halfway across Mim's expansive front yard, Sadie halted in her tracks, bowed her head and allowed herself to fully submit to her Heavenly Father. "You've loved me since You created me," she whispered as peace surrounded her, releasing her fear and loneliness to Him. "Thy will be done, Lord."

Putting on her bravest face and comforted by the presence of her Heavenly Father, Sadie marched toward the barnyard where Isaac's buggy was coming to a halt. Whatever happened next, she knew that she had indeed found true love, even if it wasn't coming from Isaac.

Chapter Nineteen

❧

As Sadie approached Isaac's buggy, she breathed a sigh of relief. Isaac hadn't seen her while unhitching Shadow from the rig. He'd led the animal toward the entrance of the barn, then was promptly swallowed up by the large structure and disappeared from sight.

When his *mamm* stepped out of the buggy, Sadie almost couldn't believe her eyes. Ruth looked more contented and healthy than Sadie had ever seen her. Perhaps while focused on her own pain, Sadie hadn't noticed that Ruth had put on some weight and no longer seemed so frail and gaunt. If she hadn't been paying attention, Sadie could have easily mistaken the woman for someone else.

"Hi, Ruth! You're looking so well," Sadie gushed as they approached one another. "Don't think I've ever seen so much sunshine in your face!" Sadie gestured toward the clear plastic shopping bag that Ruth held in one hand. "I know you went to the bulk foods store, but it looks like you purchased some fabric at a dry goods store too. Seems like you had a nice, full afternoon."

Ruth smiled broadly and nodded. She took Sadie's hand and started for the house, probably wanting to show Sadie everything she'd bought during her outing.

"I'm awful sorry, I can't right now. I need to talk to Isaac as soon as possible," Sadie protested, not allowing Ruth to guide her toward Mim's large farmhouse.

Ruth stopped in her tracks and turned to Sadie, studying her young friend with a puzzled expression. She'd undoubtedly picked up on the unfamiliar bleak tone in Sadie's voice.

Feeling her eyes start to water, Sadie cleared her throat to keep her tears at bay. "I really enjoyed all the time we spent together," she confessed just above a whisper, hoping that Isaac's *mamm* would understand just how sincerely she was loved.

Ruth's brow furrowed as she continued to gawk at Sadie. With motherly concern evident across her face, her lips parted and she took in a breath as if she was about to say something.

"Sadie! I didn't know you were here." Sadie spun around to see Isaac, who had emerged from the barn. His mocha eyes twinkled with nervous expectation and he looked her up and down like he couldn't believe she was real. "It's real *gut* to see you."

"We need to talk," Sadie sighed, anguished by Isaac's tender words. She turned back to face Ruth. "I'll see you at the next church gathering." She smiled weakly, nodding reassuringly to emphasize how much she cherished their special connection.

Ruth's grimace couldn't hide her worry. She reached for Sadie's hand and gave it a few supportive squeezes before turning and slowly heading toward the house.

"Wanna take a walk to Mill Creek? I'm sure Mim won't mind if you borrow her fishing pole." Isaac grinned down at Sadie as if her sudden appearance was the highlight of his day.

Did he believe that everything was right as rain between them, just because she'd sought him out to talk?

Sadie shook her head. "*Nee*, not today." She knew it wasn't a good idea. Once she said what she had to say, she would want to leave as quickly as possible. No sense dragging out the awkward, heart-wrenching moment. She glanced at the house and spotted both Ruth and Mim standing on the porch, their necks craned toward the barnyard. "Could we go into the barn to talk?"

"*Jah*, of course," Isaac agreed, his broad smile beginning to droop. "After you." He motioned, allowing Sadie to step into the barn first. The pair went deep into the mostly empty barn and turned toward the cow stalls. Mim's two Holsteins were outside grazing, leaving Isaac and Sadie totally alone for their private conversation.

"Seems like it's been a long time since we've seen each other," Isaac suddenly declared, charging at the elephant in the room. "I've been thinking about you a lot over the past two weeks."

Sadie now knew that he was aware something was wrong, and that he'd decided to avoid unnecessary small talk. She stared at the ground as she walked beside Isaac, unable to meet his gaze. "I've been thinking about you as well."

Isaac abruptly stopped in his tracks and turned his body to face her. "I've also been thinking about the day of the birthday party, and I know that was the day that you started distancing yourself from me." He paused, studying Sadie with imploring eyes. "What happened between us when we went for that walk in the rain?"

Sadie knew the answer to that question. They had shared an unexpected, perfect kiss, and afterward, Sadie had realized that she was in love with a man she could never have, a man who'd specifically mentioned several times that he would never allow himself to love another woman.

"Sadie?"

Unable to rally the strength to answer Isaac's query, Sadie collected herself. She lifted her eyes to meet Isaac's. "We need to end our courtship."

Isaac took a step back as if he was in shock. "What? We agreed to court for six months. It hasn't even been half that long yet."

Sadie mustered a half-hearted shrug. She gazed up at the rafters, noticing a barn swallow leave its nest and swoop out of the barn, wishing she could fly away with it. "*Jah*, well…things have changed. Better to end it now before things get more complicated than they already are."

Isaac let out a loud scoff before he threw his hands in the air. "What's changed? What's so complicated? You and I have always been close, and I see no reason why we can't just move forward with the way things are!"

Sadie blinked against threatening tears. "Please don't make this difficult, Isaac." A wave of nausea brewed throughout her middle, the gut-wrenching good-bye making bile rise in her throat. "I wish you, your *mamm*…all of you…the very best." Unable to face the man who she was certain was her soul mate for a moment longer, Sadie spun and dashed toward the barn's exit.

"Sadie! Wait just a minute, will you?" Isaac dashed after her, keeping hot on her heels. "You know how much I care about you! Please tell me what's got you so upset! Was it our kiss?"

Hearing Isaac's clomping footsteps behind her, and his direct question, Sadie stopped in her tracks, which sent Isaac nearly crashing into her.

"I don't want to pretend anymore!" The truthful explanation had come out in a near shout. Sadie stood as still as a statue for several moments, somewhat embarrassed by her outburst but also nearly relieved that she'd given Isaac some vague insight into her emotions. She couldn't pretend to be his sweetheart when she truly loved him with every bit of her being.

Glancing over her shoulder at Isaac, who stood behind her, mouth agape and clearly stunned speechless, Sadie stepped out of the barn and out of Isaac's world.

After a completely restless night, caring for the animals at dawn and picking at the breakfast that Mim forced him to eat, Isaac dashed to the barn to get Shadow. His hands shook as he hitched the horse to his buggy, and he nearly misplaced his footing and fell hard on the ground when he scrambled to get into the carriage. He was on an urgent mission, and there was no time to waste.

Yesterday's shocking conversation with Sadie had turned his world upside down. He knew that something had been troubling her, but he'd been absolutely dismayed that she was upset enough to part ways. And all of this after they'd shared what he'd thought to be a loving kiss. Sure, he'd taken a huge risk by initiating the tender moment, but Sadie had returned a gentle kiss of her own. Had she realized that she had no romantic feelings toward him after all and panicked since they were technically a couple? Isaac's frazzled mind explored that and several other possibilities as he slapped the reins and rushed his horse out onto the road, ignoring the rattling of the buggy as it sped down the lane.

What was he going to say to Sadie when he arrived at her house? Even if he was able to articulate just how desperately he needed her back in his life, Sadie might just interpret whatever he said as only meaningless words. Besides, after yesterday's visit, she might not even be willing to hear him out. Still, Isaac knew that he had to try.

When Isaac pulled his buggy into the Stolzfus barnyard, he wasted no time in his search for Sadie. "Anyone home?" he called out. He strained to hear if anyone returned his urgent greeting, though it was almost impossible to detect anything over Shadow's hoof stomping and labored breathing.

When Isaac hollered again, he was relieved to see Mose peek out of the barn. "I was expecting to see you sometime this week," he cheerfully announced as he approached Isaac's buggy, a peppy spring in his step.

Isaac's already rapid heartbeat intensified. "Why's that?" he asked anxiously, pulling back on Shadow's reins as the animal urged forward, still energized from the race to the Stolzfus farm.

Mose's brows drew together. "Well, because Sadie's been in better spirits this morning." Mose's welcoming smile suddenly faded. "Figured you two had worked things out."

Isaac shook his head, or at least he thought he did. Both his mind and body seemed paralyzed. Mose was still talking, but Isaac was unable to hear what his friend was saying. In any other circumstance, Isaac would be glad to know that Sadie was feeling better after a period of gloominess. But this…this was different. First, she'd terminated their feigned relationship, and now her brother was saying that her melancholy mood had suddenly lifted like a spring fog. Riddled with guilt, Isaac shuddered and hung his head. Was Sadie better off without him?

Once Isaac realized that he was in love with Sadie, he'd always assumed that her best interests would be at the front of his mind. But what if that meant she would be happier, more at peace, without his presence? Her tone in yesterday's conversation made it sound like she didn't even want to continue their friendship. Isaac had raced to the Stolzfuses' farm without a speck of doubt that he was willing to fight for Sadie, for her love. But was he willing to walk away, if that's what was best for her?

"You *oll recht*, Isaac? You're looking mighty pale."

"Where is she?" Isaac's question sounded more like a demand, disregarding Mose's concern for his wellness.

Mose jerked his head toward the house. "She was around back of the house, in her garden, last time I saw her."

"Hold these," Isaac muttered as he handed the reins to Mose and stumbled out of his buggy.

Like a newborn colt standing for the first time, Isaac's legs were unsteady as he started toward the impressive two-story stone house. His speed picked up as he rounded the side of the Stolzfus home, and by the time he reached the immaculately kept backyard, he was running as fast as his legs could carry him. There was Sadie, pretty as ever, kneeling near a large patch of dirt where she appeared to be planting several yellow mums. Unable to slow the beating of his heart or the pounding of his feet against the ground, Isaac charged for the garden. He was galloping toward his future, knowing that this conversation would change his life forever. One way or another.

"Sadie!" Isaac shouted as he neared the garden, feeling like his lungs were about to collapse. Sadie flinched and looked up from her work, apparently startled by Isaac's sudden, loud appearance. "I wasn't happy with how our conversation ended yesterday," Isaac panted as he struggled to catch his breath. He waited on pins and needles for Sadie's response, half expecting her to rise and flee from him.

Sadie's slight shoulders shrugged as she removed the

disposable pot from one of her mums. "Neither was I, but it was time to let you know what was on my mind."

Surprised by her unruffled response, Isaac watched Sadie in disbelief as she quietly resumed transferring her mums from their disposable containers into the rich soil. He cleared his throat, realizing that in his panic-fueled state, his tone had been far too harsh. He released an exasperated sigh before continuing. "What am I supposed to make of this? You show up after nearly two weeks of ignoring me, only to break off our courtship… our special friendship…with barely an explanation?"

Sadie didn't look up from the ground as she tucked some dirt around one of the freshly planted autumn flowers. "What do you want me to say?" Her voice quivered. She sniffled and wiped her nose on the back of her wrist.

"What do I want you to say? I want to know where we stand," Isaac pleaded, his voice rising though he did his best to control its volume. "After how close we were…after our walk in the rain…?"

Sadie glanced up at him for a fraction of a second, her vibrant green eyes matching the vivid hue of the grass that surrounded her. "I'm done faking a courtship. Thought I was pretty clear about that." She looked up at him again. Her previous stern grimace had been replaced with a tranquil expression. "I'm not mad at you or anything. I just got to thinking that it was wrong to get ourselves tangled up in a courtship for show." A small, pained smile crossed her rosy lips. "We were both suffering, albeit for different reasons. Could've saved us lots of trouble if we'd gone to the Lord instead, *jah*?"

Isaac was dumbfounded. So Sadie had indeed come to terms with her chronic singleness. She didn't need him anymore. The wisdom that flowed out of her never failed to impress him, but Sadie's wisdom wasn't what Isaac had raced to see her for. "But what does that mean for us? We were friends before I asked you to be my *aldi*."

Sadie's eyes fluttered shut. As if carefully collecting her thoughts, she took her time before answering. Though the ribbons of her *kapp* rustled in the gentle breeze, her perfect stillness reflected a new inner tranquility that Isaac envied.

When he could stand the suspense no longer, Isaac begged for an answer. "Sadie?"

"I'm done putting on a show."

Isaac stood motionless in disbelief. "But what does that mean? You've always been so direct with me, so why can't you be direct with me now? What about our friendship? You…you're the best friend I've ever had!"

Sadie said nothing as she clambered to her feet. Wiping her dirty hands on her chore apron, she gazed into the depths of Isaac's soul. "You were my best friend too." She inhaled deeply, as if suppressing a heavy sadness. "Excuse me." She brushed past him, the scent of her lavender soap lingering behind her even after she left the garden.

"So that's it," Isaac grilled her, following in her footsteps as she headed toward the house. "You're done with me?"

Sadie stopped and spun around so abruptly that Isaac almost stepped on the back of her sneakers. "I'm done…

putting…on…a…show." She said the words slowly and firmly, like she was filled with conviction. "I told you yesterday…I can't pretend anymore!"

"Is this really what you want?" Isaac reached out for her mud-stained hand, catching it as she bounded up the porch stairs.

Isaac expected Sadie to pull her hand away, but she didn't. "No, but I've prayed for peace and understanding, and my prayers were answered."

Well, there it was. Sadie, although still mourning something, was all right. She appeared far more serious than the Sadie he'd first met that rainy day in the greenhouse parking lot. She certainly wasn't happy, but she'd managed to find a hint of peace amid the chaos of their relationship, the chaos he'd created by suggesting a phony courtship in the first place.

A bittersweet flood of emotions washed over Isaac. There was immense relief in seeing that Sadie was on the mend. On the other hand, he felt himself succumbing to an intense grief that he'd prayed to never battle again. When he released Sadie's hand, Isaac's stomach soured as he came to grips with the realization this touch had been their last. *Sadie, I love you so much that I'll let you go,* he confessed inwardly.

Doing his best to keep his emotions in check, Isaac swallowed against the lump in his throat. How was he supposed to say farewell to the woman who'd mended his spirit and given him a second chance at love? His world had been shattered when Rebecca had died, and now its pieces were smashed beyond recognition because he'd lost Sadie too. Several silent moments passed before Isaac was able to assemble some parting words. "Well, we had a good run."

Sadie's head bobbed and she sniffled several more times as she glanced down at Isaac from her spot up on the porch. "*Jah*, the best."

Isaac reached to rub the back of his neck. "I'll see you around, I guess." He quickly turned to leave, not sure if he would be able to bear hearing Sadie's lovely voice bidding him farewell.

"Isaac?"

He turned on his heels, his vision becoming blurry with unshed tears. Sadie stood beneath the doorframe, halfway into the large farmhouse. Halfway out of his life. "*Jah?*" he questioned, fearing that his voice would fail him.

"I'll always love you."

The otherwise comforting words were anything but a balm to soothe his wounded spirit. The love of friendship wasn't enough. Unsure of how to respond, Isaac decided that a small dose of honesty couldn't hurt. "I'll always love you too."

Deciding that there was nothing left to say, Isaac turned again and plodded to the barnyard. Mose was no longer in sight. He'd probably retreated somewhere deep within the barn to allow his sister and her visitor as much privacy as possible. Isaac valued Mose's kind consideration, especially now that he doubted he'd want to make conversation ever again.

Isaac carelessly flung himself into his rig. Taking the buggy's brake off and limply picking up the reins, he clicked his tongue to get Shadow moving. The horse started with a lazy walk, and Isaac allowed his snail's pace to continue since he was in no hurry to go anywhere. What was the point, especially when Sadie was no longer by his side?

The future was beyond grim. Unfortunately for Isaac, the loss of love had become all too familiar. He'd survived it once, but how would he carry on now that his heart had been shattered for a second time? Sadie had been a blessing from *Gott*, appearing in his life when he'd needed her most. In the privacy of his buggy and with only Shadow to hear, Isaac gave in to the tears that had built up since the day of the birthday party. He wept bitterly as Shadow clopped down the lane, away from Sadie, away from his closest friend, and the soul he desperately loved.

Chapter Twenty

"Another rainy day."

Isaac glanced toward the screen door from his seat on one of the porch rocking chairs. There was Mim, grinning compassionately at him from behind the mesh door. Not in the mood for conversation, Isaac nodded and returned his focus to the water that was splashing down from the eaves above. He'd been sitting there staring at the rain for at least an hour, if not two, but the time spent with only his thoughts for company had been anything but peaceful.

Mim opened the creaking screen door, stepped outside and took a seat next to her nephew. "You've been sitting here since breakfast, and now it's almost time for the noon meal." One of her wispy eyebrows climbed higher than the other. "How's a person supposed to work up an appetite just sitting around all day?"

"Please, Mim." Isaac rubbed small circles into his temples. He was certain that his aunt was only teasing, but his soul ached something terrible and even her jolly, playful banter wasn't enough to make him crack a smile.

"What's your *mamm* up to? She went outside before the rain started this morning and hasn't come back inside," Mim mentioned, causing Isaac to wonder if she was trying to goad him into a conversation.

"I told her that I saw a new batch of kittens in the barn when I was feeding the animals this morning, and I think she went out to see them."

Mim let out a soft chuckle. "When she was a little *maedel*, Ruth always loved fussing over newborn animals. Seems like she takes one step toward her old self with each day that passes." She leaned forward, loosening the shawl wrapped around her shoulders. "Thought it'd be cooler out here for a late-September day. Things are starting to warm up."

"Uh-huh."

"But not warm enough to chase away the chill in your heart, *jah*?"

Isaac whipped his head in Mim's direction so quickly that his neck loudly cracked. He winced, massaging the spot that was now sore. "I guess not."

Mim smiled affectionately at him as she reached to brush a lock of sandy hair away from his eyes. "None of my business what the young folks are up to, of course, but it's plain to see that your joy seemed to disappear around the same that Sadie stopped visiting."

Isaac shuddered. Mim was absolutely correct. According to the community's tradition, her peeking into his romantic life was wildly unusual. But he felt more lost than a needle in a haystack, and if Mim had some providential words to share, who was he to stop her? He waited impatiently for his aunt to continue, watching her as she gazed into the intensifying rain shower.

"Whenever we face an impossible obstacle, the Lord has already placed the solution right in front of our nose. Sometimes we just need to open our eyes to see it." Mim stood and started toward the door. "Anyway, I'll have lunch on the table shortly. Please run and get your *mamm* in a couple of minutes, but grab some umbrellas before you do. Don't want either of you getting soaked to the bone in this weather!" With that, she retreated indoors.

Isaac harrumphed and crossed his arms over his chest. A damp breeze lapped against his skin as Mim's words rattled around his mind. What solution could there possibly be, unless Sadie loved him in return?

In an attempt to force a distraction, Isaac slapped his knees, sprang up from his chair and wandered across the porch. Leaning on the hand railing, he stared at the soggy ground, noticing for the first time that Mim had planted several yellow mums. Sadie's favorite color, Isaac reminded himself. He hung his head and chuckled at the irony. Reminders of Sadie were everywhere, all of the time.

If Mim knew about this, she'd say it was a "solution from the Lord." Isaac scoffed at the notion, but that rapidly morphed into intense reflection. Were both Mim and the Lord working together to get him to study this from another angle?

Wicking away droplets of water, Isaac skimmed his hand across the railing as he pondered this further.

Surely, if Sadie loved him, she would have given him some sort of hint. Had she been giving him clues that he'd missed?

The first memory that came to mind was of their unexpected, tender kiss. That moment had lit a fire in his heart. Had Sadie been warmed by the same spark? True, she had fled from him moments later, but before that, she'd willingly returned a soft kiss of her own.

She'd said we'd both been caught up in the moment, Isaac sternly reminded himself. She'd said we must've both thought our courtship was real. He continued gawking at the brightly colored flowers as he stood at the edge of the porch, hanging on to the railing to support himself. What did all of this add up to?

Isaac sighed as he ambled back across the porch to his empty chair. Was he just clinging to any glimmer of hope? If only Sadie knew just how much he'd come to love her.

I'll always love you.

Sadie's final words to him echoed through Isaac's mind. At the time, he'd been certain that Sadie was referring to the love one Christian has for all other people. She had a sweet spirit, so that was to be expected. But she kissed him back. She'd said she was done putting on a show. She'd said she would always love him.

Isaac dropped back into his chair with a thud, feeling like he might pass out. Sadie loved him, and he loved her! They could have a life together, a joyful, loving life! Against all odds, love had found two unlikely hearts and woven the threads of their lives together in the most complicated yet perfect way possible. During a summertime downpour, a gorgeous, quirky stranger had emerged from the rain and walked into Isaac's life, and she would become the woman he wished to marry. Now, during another rain shower, he'd come to realize that his unusual, patient, lovely best friend was his soul mate.

Isaac snapped out of his musings when he saw the barn door slide open in the distance. Mim was ringing the supper bell from the backyard. His mother must've heard its clanging and assumed that it was time for lunch. "Wait a second, *Mamm*! I'll bring you an umbrella," Isaac called, cupping his hands around his mouth to amplify his voice. He stood, but before he could turn to fetch the umbrellas, he noticed something unusual out of the corner of his eye.

As Ruth emerged from the barn, she suddenly came to a stop and turned her face up toward the sky. She smiled as raindrops landed on her face, and much to Isaac's surprise, she even stuck her tongue out to catch a few. Then, as if she hadn't a care in the world, she skipped toward an already sizeable puddle growing in a low spot on the lawn. To Isaac's total shock and complete amusement, Ruth splashed around in the puddle, kicking her bare feet through the water. She stretched out her arms and spun around as the rain drenched her clothing. Her smile widened and she let out a laugh that soon turned into a fit of giggles.

Isaac couldn't believe his eyes and ears as he stood on the porch, gawking at his *mamm*'s playful outburst. What a blessing the sound of her laughter was! It had been years since she'd last laughed. Tears rushed to his eyes as a flood of happiness and a torrent of gratefulness washed over him while the rain washed over his mother. Isaac dashed into the rain, needing to celebrate this monumental step forward in his mother's recovery.

Hearing her son's heavy footsteps splashing through puddles, Ruth stopped her spinning, though her smile was still broad enough to stretch across Lancaster County. She held her arms out to receive his embrace with the unmistakable expression of a concerned parent. When Isaac reached her, she looked into his red eyes and wiped away a tear before it could be mixed with the raindrops that pelted his face.

"It's *oll recht*, *Mamm*. I'm just so happy!" Isaac held his mother's cool hands in his, without feeling the need to hide his emotions from her for the first time since Rebecca's death. "I'm just so thankful to hear you laughing again." He sniffed, unashamed of his joyful tears. "Sadie really had an effect on both of us, *jah*?"

Ruth nodded as she held both of her son's hands in hers. "Go to her."

The moment that his mother's words left her lips, Isaac let out a delighted whoop. He embraced her so tightly that her feet left the ground. He'd nearly forgotten the calming sound of his mother's voice, and hearing it again was truly an answered prayer. For the longest time, he'd feared that he would never hear another word from her, and that anxiety had just been crushed by her three small words. Her first words, advising him to go after Sadie, put an official end to over two years of pain, misery and loneliness for both mother and son.

"Go to her," Ruth repeated, her voice cracking and shaky after not being used for years. "Go to your Sadie."

* * *

"I'm heading over to Rhoda's. Her *daed* is planning a small addition onto his workshop and I offered to lend a hand," Mose announced as he entered the kitchen with a noisy yawn and a tall stretch. "Do you wanna come with me?"

Sadie shook her head as she pulled a large plastic mixing bowl from the cupboard. "*Nee, denki.* I think I'm gonna try to bake something this afternoon."

Mose's mouth dropped open and he studied her inquisitively. "That sure doesn't sound like my twin talking."

Sadie shrugged and chuckled softly at her brother's visible shock. "*Jah*, I'm a whole new woman."

"*Ach*, no need for that! We like you just the way you are." Mose smiled, though Sadie could see the concern that was poorly hidden behind his grin. "Are you sure you don't want to come along? I know Rhoda would enjoy your company."

Sadie let out a pent-up breath. With her parents out to lunch with the *Englisch* neighbors and Susannah at the schoolhouse, she was looking forward to spending some time alone. "I love Rhoda, but I don't think I'd be good company for anyone," Sadie explained gently, hoping her brother would catch the hint.

Mose nodded sympathetically. "I gotcha." He headed for the door and explained that he would be staying at Rhoda's for dinner. He bid Sadie farewell and stepped outside only to return a few seconds later. "I can tell that something has your heart hurting awful bad, but I'm real proud of how strong you've been."

Sadie's heart was warmed by her brother's tender, supportive words. "It's strength given to me from above."

Mose agreed, and after another goodbye, he headed back outside.

Despite her best efforts to hide her gloom and carry on with life's daily activities, Sadie's broken heart was apparently still visible to others. Though she prayed daily for peace, the deep melancholy never seemed to lessen. For that reason, she'd been going out of her way to keep her mind and hands busy, reasoning that a busy person had less time to focus on her woes.

After rooting through the cabinets to see what supplies were available, Sadie decided to whip up a batch of chocolate chip cookies. It was the only recipe that she knew how to bake reasonably well, and she didn't want her efforts to be wasted on something that might turn out to be inedible anyway.

While she was mixing the dry ingredients, Sadie thought she'd spied some movement outdoors. Leaning closer to the window above the counter, she watched as the family's golden retriever bolted out of the barn and raced toward the long, tree-lined driveway. That wasn't particularly unusual. Buster had a lot of energy and enjoyed chasing squirrels and rabbits. The dog's adorable, almost goofy expression seemed quite wound-up, as it often did when a member of the family arrived home after being away for several hours. Maybe *Mamm* and *Daed* were back from the restaurant.

By the time she was pouring the chocolate chips into the mixture, she heard the sound of buggy wheels rumbling over the drumming of raindrops against the window. Now that she thought of it, it certainly wasn't her parents returning home since they'd gone to the restaurant by car. Maybe Mose had come back to fetch her at Rhoda's insistence, or maybe someone had come calling for an afternoon visit.

Sadie curiously peered out the window again and worried that her eyes might be playing a terrible trick on her. She immediately noticed the visiting horse's unusual gray coloring. The only gray buggy horse that she knew of was Shadow, who belonged to Isaac. Sadie used a nearby cloth to wipe some steam from the window. She pressed her nose against the glass pane and squinted to be absolutely sure that the scene outside wasn't just a manifestation of what her heart longed for most. Sure enough, it was Isaac sitting in his buggy, laughing as Buster jumped in to greet him.

Sadie placed a hand over her heart, trying to stop its racing. What in the world was Isaac doing here? What more was there to say? She backed away from the window, unsure if she was willing to meet her visitor. Part of her wanted to dash up the stairs to her bedroom, jump onto her bed and hide beneath her quilt until Isaac left. Taking a moment to slow her breathing, she closed her eyes and inhaled deeply. *I am never truly alone*, she reminded herself. Revitalized with the comfort of *Gott*, Sadie hurried outside without stopping to grab her shawl or umbrella.

She skipped down the porch steps and darted across the lawn, unable to dodge the raindrops as she made her way toward the barnyard to help Isaac unhitch Shadow and settle the animal in the barn.

As she approached the buggy, Buster stuck his head out of the rig at the sound of her hurried steps through the puddles. With his tongue lolling and tail wagging, he let out a woof and hopped out of the buggy. Sadie scratched the dog behind his damp ears, taking comfort in the faithful canine's affection.

The buggy creaked a bit as Isaac clambered out of it, his masculine but gentle features nearly stopping Sadie's heart. For a moment, they stared at each other through the rain, neither one of them speaking. Though Sadie hated to admit it, it was tremendously wonderful to see Isaac again.

Pushing away the longing that she knew would never fully leave her, Sadie noticed that Isaac was completely drenched, as if he'd been standing in the rain for far longer than these few moments. "You're downright soaked."

Isaac looked down at his sopping shirt, the movement of his head causing all of the water atop his hat to rush to the brim. "It's raining, just like the day we met, *jah*?" Isaac studied her with a look she hadn't seen from him since the day of the birthday party. "My…uh…my *mamm* started speaking again today."

Sadie immediately felt tears rush to her eyes. Were they brought on by seeing Isaac again, or from the happy news that Ruth had fully recovered from her condition? "*Ach*, that's *wunderbar*." She nodded, feeling her warm tears mix with the cool September raindrops on her flushed cheeks.

Isaac took a step forward but then seemed to hesitate. "It is *wunderbar!*" He stared at the ground, the brim of his hat hiding his face.

"Why did you come here?" Sadie asked him point-blank.

Isaac turned toward Shadow, running his hand along the horse's back, which sent even more water droplets flying through the air. "I can't be without you by my side."

Sadie tilted her head, fearful that she would mis-interpret what Isaac was conveying. "We can be friends again."

"No," Isaac retorted almost immediately as he rushed closer to her, now just inches away. "How can I be only friends with the woman who changed my life, who makes me feel truly alive, even after I thought my spirit was dead?" He reached for her hand, then pulled her close enough for her to feel his heartbeat. "I love the woman who chases lightning bugs and who bakes the strangest cookies I've ever seen." His eyes shone brighter than the harvest moon on a crystal clear night. "I love the woman who eats pies like an apple and who brings joy to every life that she touches. I love you, Sadie, and I want you to be my wife."

With her cheek pressed against his chest, Sadie was unable to control her tears of joy. Her heart had found a home, and it was warm and welcoming. Isaac con-tinued to hold her, resting his head on top of hers while she wept.

Finally, Sadie managed to compose herself. She looked up, causing the beating rain to wash away her tears as a lifetime of loneliness was rinsed away as well. "I love you too, Isaac! I can't wait to be your wife."

Smiling down at her, Isaac kissed Sadie's damp forehead and then each of her cheeks. Sliding his hand under her chin, he tilted her face upward. Their lips met, and for the first time in her life, Sadie felt like she was home. When their lips parted, Isaac embraced her again. "Sadie Stolzfus," he whispered in her ear, his cheek pressed against hers, "you taught me to love the rain."

Epilogue

"I must say, I can't remember ever baking fourteen pies in a single morning," Mim stated as she shoved her hands into her quilted oven mitts. She opened the door of her oven, reached inside and pulled out two apple-crumble pies that looked like they could have been featured on the cover of a cookbook.

Sadie studied the previous dozen pies, all of which stood cooling, lined up like ducklings across Mim's counter. "I can't remember ever making something that looks so *appenditlich*!"

Mim chortled as she placed the last two pies on the end of the counter. "They do look delicious! You've been practicing a lot lately, and I'm sure everyone will enjoy these pies at Mose and Rhoda's wedding tomorrow." Mim took off her oven mitts, then hung them on their designated hook on the wall. She moved to the sink and stopped to peer out of the small window above the faucet. "Looks like a car just pulled in and someone's getting out of it with several suitcases." She craned her neck toward Sadie and issued her a mischievous grin. "I reckon it's a taxi bringing someone from the bus station in Lancaster. Wonder who that could be?"

Knowing that Isaac was to return from his trip to Indiana, Sadie let out a squeal and charged out the door. Isaac had traveled to Shipshewana with his mother several weeks ago. Once his mother was settled in back home, Isaac had planned to pack up all of his belongings and return to Bird-in-Hand, though this time he would be returning for good.

"*Willkumm* home!" Sadie shouted as she threw her arms around Isaac's neck. He dropped his suitcases and wrapped Sadie in a warm embrace, which felt so loving that it nearly brought tears to her eyes.

Isaac lifted her off the ground and spun her in several tight circles, causing both of them to laugh.

"*Ach*, it's *gut* to be back in Lancaster County," Isaac declared as he placed Sadie on the ground. "Indiana certainly doesn't feel like home anymore."

"*Jah*, and you're back just in time to see Mose and Rhoda get married tomorrow, though I'm sorry your *mamm* will miss the wedding," Sadie replied, feeling a hint of disappointment. She'd missed Ruth ever since she'd left Bird-in-Hand, though she knew she would see her future mother-in-law again someday.

"Well, I've got some exciting news to share," Isaac replied with one of the biggest smiles that Sadie had ever seen. "*Mamm*, *Daed* and all of my unmarried sisters are moving to Lancaster County as well. *Daed* is coming into town next week and he and I are going house hunting for them. Then we'll find a shop for rent, where he can run his woodworking business from."

"That's *wunderbar*," Sadie exclaimed, clapping her hands together. "I can't wait to meet the rest of your family."

Isaac's grin fairly sparkled as he and Sadie each picked up one of his suitcases and headed toward a nearby bench that rested beneath a weeping willow tree. "You should've heard *Mamm* excitedly talking *Daed*'s ear off about how successful his business will be with all the Lancaster tourists stopping by. Truth be told, it doesn't matter what *Mamm* talks about. We're all simply overjoyed just to hear her voice again."

"The Lord has a way of working everything out," Sadie mused with a pleasant sigh. She and Isaac took a seat on the bench, and Isaac promptly draped his arm around her shoulders, as if to protect her from the chilly November breeze.

"You've got that right," Isaac agreed as he pulled Sadie to sit closer to him. "Mim's generous offer to pass on the farm and house to us was another blessing that I never expected, and I'm awful glad that you managed to convince her to continue living here even after we're married next month."

Sadie snuggled closer to Isaac and rested her head against his shoulder. "Imagine the day, not so far away, when you'll be working the farm, I'll be tending to the flower beds and our children will be listening to one of Mim's famous stories."

Isaac nodded contentedly and rested his cheek on

top of Sadie's head. "If that isn't a happily-ever-after, I don't know what is. How did I get to be so lucky?"

Sadie smiled so widely that her cheeks ached, feeling her heartbeat fall into sync with Isaac's. "I don't think it has anything to do with luck. I believe the Lord led us to each other."

Isaac gently turned Sadie's face up to his. He planted a heart-stopping kiss on her lips before gazing into her eyes with a love that few people ever truly find. "I'll love you forever, Sadie, come rain or shine."

* * * * *

Dear Reader,

I am thrilled to share this story of hope, love and redemption with you! Sadie and Isaac's story is a very special tale, and I think many people can relate to the emotions that both characters experience.

Lancaster County has always been close to my heart, and I've been writing Amish books since I was eleven years old. This story is my first Love Inspired book to hit the shelves, and I am over-the-moon excited to transport readers to Amish Country, where life moves at a slower pace.

I'd love to connect with you! You're welcome to visit my Facebook page, Jackie Stef's Plain & Fancy. I'll be posting book news and connecting with readers there, as well as sharing my personal photography from Amish Country. Feel free to send me a message!

Thank you for reading my story!
Blessings and Peace,

Jackie Stef

WE HOPE YOU ENJOYED
THIS BOOK FROM

LOVE INSPIRED
INSPIRATIONAL ROMANCE

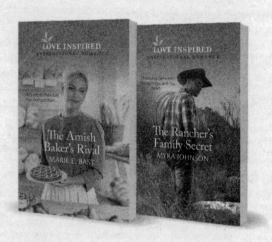

Uplifting stories of faith, forgiveness and hope.

Fall in love with stories where faith helps
guide you through life's challenges, and discover
the promise of a new beginning.

6 NEW BOOKS AVAILABLE EVERY MONTH!

COMING NEXT MONTH FROM
Love Inspired

THE AMISH MATCHMAKING DILEMMA
Amish Country Matches • by Patricia Johns

Amish bachelor Mose Klassen wants a wife who is quiet and traditional—the exact opposite of his childhood friend Naomi Peachy. But when she volunteers as his speech tutor, Mose can't help but be drawn to the outgoing woman. Could an unexpected match be his perfect fit?

TRUSTING HER AMISH HEART
by Cathy Liggett

Leah Zook finds purpose caring for the older injured owner of an Amish horse farm—until his estranged son returns home looking for redemption. The mysterious Zach Graber has all the power to fix the run-down farm—and Leah's locked-down heart. But together will they be strong enough to withstand his secret?

A REASON TO STAY
K-9 Companions • by Deb Kastner

Suddenly responsible for a brother she never knew about, Emma Fitzgerald finds herself out of her depth in a small Colorado town. But when cowboy Sharpe Winslow and his rescue pup, Baloo, take the troubled boy under their wing, Emma can't resist growing close to them and maybe finding a reason to stay...

THE COWGIRL'S REDEMPTION
Hope Crossing • by Mindy Obenhaus

Gloriana Prescott has returned to her Texas ranch to make amends—even if the townsfolk she left behind aren't ready to forgive. But when ranch manager Justin Broussard must save the struggling rodeo, Gloriana sees a chance to prove she's really changed. But can she show Justin, and the town, that she's trustworthy?

FINDING HER VOICE
by Donna Gartshore

Bridget Connelly dreams of buying her boss's veterinary clinic—and so does Sawyer Blume. But it's hard to stay rivals when Sawyer's traumatized daughter bonds with Bridget's adorable pup. When another buyer places a bid, working together might give them everything they want...including each other.

ONCE UPON A FARMHOUSE
by Angie Dicken

Helping her grandmother sell the farm and escaping back to Chicago are all Molly Jansen wants—not to reunite with her ex, single father and current tenant farmer Jack Behrens. But turning Jack and his son out—and not catching feelings for them—might prove more difficult than she realized...

LOOK FOR THESE AND OTHER LOVE INSPIRED BOOKS WHEREVER BOOKS ARE SOLD, INCLUDING MOST BOOKSTORES, SUPERMARKETS, DISCOUNT STORES AND DRUGSTORES.

LICNM0722

"I'm not easy to match, and I know it," she replied. "My sister is a matchmaker and even she had trouble with me. That should tell you something. Maybe it's why I want to drag some *Englishers* into our midst."

His stomach dropped, and he shot her a look of surprise.

"T-to marry?" he asked.

"No!" Naomi rolled her eyes. "But next to a bunch of *Englishers*, I'm downright safe, you know?"

"Yah." He wasn't so fortunate, though. Standing him next to *Englishers* wouldn't fix what made him different.

"I'm joking, of course. But I do give that impression, don't I?" Naomi asked with a sigh.

"What?" he asked.

"Of being a rebellious woman, of wanting to jump the fence," she said. "I don't think I'm actually so different from the other women—I just don't hide things as well! They're better at keeping their thoughts to themselves, and mine come out of my mouth before I think better of them."

LIEXP0722

"That's…a blessing," he said. At least she was honest.

Naomi put the pitchfork down with a clank of metal against concrete floor. "We're polar opposites, you and me, Mose. I talk too fast, and you aren't able to say everything in your head."

Mose met her gaze. "It's h-hard being d-d-different."

"Amen to that," she murmured. Then she smiled. "But a good friend helps."

Yah, a good friend did help. With Naomi and her wild hair and even wilder way of thinking, he didn't feel so alone—she'd always had that effect on him.

But she was right—Naomi was an example of why the *Ordnung* was so important. Everyone needed to be reined in, given boundaries, made to pause and think. Because if everyone just swung off after their own inclinations, there wouldn't be any Amish community anymore. Everything they valued—the togetherness, the simplicity, the traditions—would be nothing but a memory.

But looking at Naomi, catching her glittering green eyes, he couldn't be the one to hold her back. He could try, but in the end, he wouldn't be able to do it because she'd always been his weakness.

Mose felt his face heat and he wheeled the barrow off toward the door to dump it. She was helping him get more comfortable with talking. That was all. And he'd best remember it.

Don't miss
The Amish Matchmaking Dilemma *by Patricia Johns,*
available September 2022
wherever Love Inspired books and ebooks are sold.

LoveInspired.com

IF YOU ENJOYED THIS BOOK, DON'T MISS NEW EXTENDED-LENGTH NOVELS FROM LOVE INSPIRED!

In addition to the Love Inspired books you know and love, we're excited to introduce even more uplifting stories in a longer format, with more inspiring fresh starts and page-turning thrills!

LOVE INSPIRED

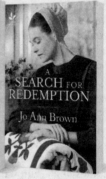

Stories to uplift and inspire.

Fall in love with Love Inspired—inspirational and uplifting stories of faith and hope. Find strength and comfort in the bonds of friendship and community. Revel in the warmth of possibility, and the promise of new beginnings.

LOOK FOR THESE LOVE INSPIRED TITLES ONLINE AND IN THE BOOK DEPARTMENT OF YOUR FAVORITE RETAILER!